TIGER DAUGHTER

REBECCA LIM

DELACORTE PRESS

Text copyright © 2021 by Rebecca Lim
Jacket illustrations from iStockphoto
Interior illustrations copyright © 2021 by Leni Liu, Yvette Liu, and Rebecca Lim

Visit us on the Web! rhcbooks.com
Educators and librarians, for a variety of teaching tools,
visit us at RHTeachersLibrarians.com

Library of Congress Cataloging-in-Publication Data is available upon request.
ISBN 978-0-593-64897-1 (trade)—ISBN 978-0-593-64898-8 (lib. bdg.)—
ISBN 978-0-593-64899-5 (ebook)

The text of this book is set in 12.75-point Chaparral Pro.
Interior design by Megan Shortt

Printed in the United States of America
10 9 8 7 6 5 4 3 2 1
First Edition

To my son and daughters,
each of whom I'm raising in their
own image, and no one else's

In this novel, references to the Chinese language are to Mandarin Chinese unless otherwise indicated. Hundreds of dialects or languages are spoken today in modern China, and people whose families emigrated from there often speak more than one of them.

CONTENTS

PROLOGUE

THE DAY BEFORE THINGS WERE NEVER THE SAME AGAIN

AS WE TAKE OUR PLACES IN THE CLASSROOM, Mr. Cornish writes with a flourish on the whiteboard, *What is the essence of being "Australian"?*

"At least a hundred words!" he says brightly, turning to face us. "In complete sentences. No shopping lists. Kon, I'm looking at you."

Kon's mouth turns down at the corners.

"Can't I just write *Whatever*?" Henry hisses in Chinese out of the side of his mouth.

Henry Xiao and I are sitting at the back of the before-school, extra English catch-up class that our school runs for refugee and migrant kids. I don't need to be here—even though I might look like I do—but my best friend Henry does. I'm only here to provide him with moral support and general translation services.

Mr. Cornish has just set another inspirational writing task in a long line of perky questions about Australian customs and sayings, and Henry's right. *Whatever,* summed up by the Chinese words suí biàn—meaning casual, random, *whatevs*—would be a completely appropriate answer to the question on the whiteboard. But I know it wouldn't be enough for Mr. Cornish, who's got so much bushranger beard going on that when he says things like "More, Henry, I need *more!*" just about no one in the room can understand him. Especially not Henry. Which is exactly why I'm here.

A one-word answer isn't going to improve anyone's language skills, or mood, this morning, so I shake my head at Henry now. "Won't cut it," I murmur, pointedly, in English, which Henry knows he should be speaking the minute he sets foot on school grounds.

"And *that* is the whole problem with this language, Wen," Henry mutters back in defiant Chinese. "*What* am I cutting? For *whom* am I cutting it?"

Henry's classified as *straight off the boat* by horrible Billy Raum. Billy believes that anyone who does their homework is a danger to society, and that people who can't play football are genetically abnormal and should've been left, like weak Spartan babies, to die of exposure on a lonely hillside. I know this because he's said so to my face. Right after he called me *slant eyes.*

Not that my eyes slant, actually. Not that it should matter, if they did.

"Is there a problem, Wen?" Mr. Cornish says to me now. I shrug in apology. Both he and I know that he's doing me—and Henry—a favor by letting me even attend this class.

"How is he able to produce those noises without moving his lips?" Henry whispers in Chinese, with fascination.

"And if you have something to say, Henry Xiao"—Mr. Cornish swivels his abundant facial hair back in Henry's direction—"you can say it to the whole class, please."

Henry screws up his face, and replies laboriously in his painfully literal English, "With sincerest apologies, I am bringing you inconvenience."

There's a short pause in the room, like a held breath, and then everyone bursts out laughing, even Mr. Cornish. The room rings with it. Henry flushes red—*whoosh*—from his ratty T-shirt collar right up to his hairline. He's like a glowing stop sign.

"You sound like my *father*!" Josip Kovačević laughs, not in a mean way. But Henry rises from his chair, grabbing all his books and pens with shaking hands.

I stop laughing. I get the feeling that people have laughed at Henry for most of his life and that one of his dearest wishes, when he grows up, is for that never to happen again.

I don't think Henry is looked after much, at home. He hardly ever has any lunch. I give him some of mine when I can spare it, and Miss Spencer and the other teachers arrange for him—and the other kids whose parents can't afford lunch, or don't remember to feed them—to have a sneaky sandwich from the school cafeteria at least three times a week. Henry's this pale, skinny kid with a bad haircut, terrible plastic-framed spectacles, and trousers so short his ankles are always showing.

Mr. Cornish sees my steadying hand on the frayed cuff of Henry's sleeve and stops laughing as well. "It's my turn to offer sincerest apologies, Henry," Mr. Cornish says gently, "but you need to find a happy medium between what you just said—*I'm sorry* would have been enough in that context—and the one-word answers you usually like to give."

Henry sits back down abruptly, something clearly having piqued his interest. He mutters to me in Chinese as Mr. Cornish turns towards the whiteboard, "I understand the meaning of *happy*, but *medium* can mean many things, Wen—a person who speaks with the dead, an art form, an average, a substance—what is he talking about with this use of the word *medium*?"

"Average, balance," I murmur out of the side of my mouth. "As in *happy balance*. He wants you to find a happy balance when you speak in class."

When you speak at all, I almost say, but don't.

Wanting to add, *You just need to* speak, *Hen. It does get easier.*

"Ah," Henry says brightly. "I will use this term in our forthcoming entrance exam. *Happy medium,* this is good."

"Uh," I begin. "About that exam we're supposed to be taking . . ."

"Do not jinx us!" Henry says sharply, for once in word-perfect English, and I close my mouth with a snap at the expression on his face. Mr. Cornish looks around at us, frowning, before turning back to the whiteboard.

Henry has this crazy idea that if we both sit the entrance exam to this amazing, government-funded selective school next month, we'll get everything we ever wanted, and our lives will change for the better. Our form teacher, Miss Spencer, told our whole class about the exam, and the school, but we're the only two kids who can be bothered doing it because the place sounds like an impossible mirage. It's on the other side of town, but it might as well be on the other side of the world.

Henry's insisting that we'll both get through with flying colors, and that the excellent science and maths program (for him) and the outstanding arts, athletics and humanities program (for me) will mean that we'll become the people we're supposed to be—instead of being two migrant kids living an hour's train ride out of the city (on a good day) in a suburb that's known in the newspapers for its homeless people, drug deals and gang violence. It's so bad here that Mom still walks me to and from school every day, even though I'm almost fourteen, and taller than she is. There's nothing beautiful about where we live except for the friends I've made at school, like Nikki Kuol and Fatima Salah, whose families come from opposite ends of Sudan and who'd probably not be friends if they still lived there, instead of here. If we'd never come to Australia, I wouldn't have known them either. So this school is the safest place in my life, and Henry's, and I'm not sure I want to leave it.

"What if we don't get *in*?" I keep my voice very quiet. "What if Miss Spencer's wrong about us being ready?"

"Miss Spencer used to teach there," Henry reminds me under his breath. "She only left because her mother got too sick to look after herself. Miss Spencer says that we'll love it there. That it has everything. That we'll fit right in, remember?"

He gets a faraway look in his eye and I know he's thinking about the gleaming new two-story library we saw in the brochure in Miss Spencer's office that also talked about the debating and fencing teams, the robotics club, the performing arts centre and the biennial space camps at NASA.

I look at Henry, whose long-sleeved T-shirt is so stretched and wash-faded and threadbare that it looks like a ghost garment, then look down at me, in my too-tight school sweatshirt, and jeans that are about to bust out in holes around the bum area. The denim is so thin that people will be able to make out the color of my underpants any moment now. I don't ever feel I can ask for anything new, so I don't ask; until someone, eventually, notices that my clothes are so tight or so short or so scandalous that I look like a sausage busting rudely out of its skin, and one new garment may suddenly appear at the end of my bed. Just one; so that I don't get ideas. From a seconds warehouse somewhere; the kind filled with racks of clothing in shades of apricot, grey and aqua that are all marked $5.

For a moment, I do feel longing for a place that will make me become a better version of me. But unlike Henry, I don't feel like there is such a place, or that it can ever come true. What I feel most days is that nothing is ever going to change. That my life won't even *start,* and I'll be stuck like this forever.

"My parents will never let me go to that school," I whisper. "I have to lie to my dad just to keep you company in this English Enrichment class, remember? He thinks I'm coming here for my own personal 'enrichment.' If he knew I was only coming here for *you*, that would be it. No more class. I'm not allowed to have friends, or 'fun.' I can't even leave the house if I'm not with him, or with Mom. I don't think I'll be able to so much as sit the exam, let alone ever go to that school. It's wrong for you to even put the idea in my head, Henry Xiao."

"People who come out of that school can do anything, and be anything," Henry insists, and is only prevented from continuing by the bell that signals morning roll call.

The look I give him says *Don't be so sure.*

Mr. Cornish stops the two of us before we leave the classroom. "Henry," he says, his voice serious. "Life is about taking risks. The more you do it, the easier it will become, okay? Don't be afraid that people will laugh, and don't"—he gives me a shrewd glance—"stay inside that comfortable shell you've built around yourself. That shell, Henry, is an illusion. *To live is to risk everything*," he finishes grandly, twirling his mustache at one end.

I study Mr. Cornish, with his oiled beard and trendy new plaid shirt, dark pants, sockless shiny leather loafers and nice sporty silver car that drives him away at

3:57 every afternoon. We're just the start of his teaching "journey"—Miss Spencer said so. We're the difficult stepping-stone Mr. Cornish must jump from to reach a place in some inner-east private school for rich kids. I wonder if he really believes what he's just said, or if it's just something catchy he's read somewhere.

Mr. Cornish, fresh out of teachers' college, wilts a little as we walk out without a word.

He doesn't understand that every day Henry and I are alive, there is no comfortable shell and we are always at risk. It's in the air we breathe, it's in our bones, and people like Mr. Cornish have *Absolutely. No. Idea.*

PART ONE

The Master said, "The gentleman hates not
leaving behind a name when he is gone."

—Confucius, *The Analects*, Book XV, 20

CHAPTER 1

SMALL
MISFORTUNES

WHEN MY FRIENDS ASK ME WHAT MY LIFE HAS
been like so far, mostly I remember the rage.

Like the time last year when I wrote a letter to my
aunt in China—the youngest one on my mom's side,
the kind one—about how my dad is so strict that I'm
never allowed to go to my friends' birthday parties.
Somehow, the letter got returned while I was at school,
and Dad opened it—even though it had *my* name on it,
not his—and read it.

Then he went into my bedroom, and tore down
every poster and picture and letter from friends that
I had stuck on my walls and set them all on fire in the
backyard. He stood there watching them burn to make
sure the job was done properly, Mom whispered as I

surveyed the empty walls of my bedroom with a crushing weight sitting right in the centre of me. When I got home that day, all that was left of the things I'd drawn and collected since coming to this country as a little girl was a small pile of ashes that was still warm.

I can't remember if I cried. I'm sure I did. It's a bit blurry after the part where I was made to understand that because of the letter I wrote, the pile of ashes was all that was left of my most treasured things. *Action, consequence.* There wasn't even a corner of anything I could save.

I've left my bedroom walls bare since then, because nothing feels like it will be safe or permanent anymore. I haven't even taken the blobs of Blu Tack down. What's the point?

Another time, when I tried to discuss the possibility of having ballet lessons like my friends do, straight after school in the assembly hall, Dad rolled up the Chinese newspaper he was reading and hit me across the side of the head with it for being insolent, because *There is no point to art.* Things like wanting to learn ballet, or reading for fun, or painting *Teach you nothing useful.*

And there was that time he kicked a footstool clear across the room in front of me because I really, really wanted to have a sleepover at Michaela Shand's house and I'd begged a few times too many. And the time he hit me across the back of the hands with a bamboo cane because I was rude to my mother. She'd been telling me to do some extra maths—in the spare time I had between doing rounds of extra maths, Chinese calligraphy, piano and violin—and I think I lost it, finally, and screamed at her to *Just shut up and leave me alone*, because Mom was the safer target.

She's always been the safer target.

And, well, *blam*.

Because children don't ever answer back, in my family. They don't have opinions. They don't have the right to run their mouths off. They are the property of their parents, especially if they're girls, until they are the property of their husbands and are off their parents' hands at last and for good. *(Just another mouth to feed, useless.)*

I understand that it's bad to have daughters, because your family name dies when you have daughters, and girls can't do everything that boys can. *It's a proven fact. Everyone knows that.* I've been told this so many times, I go into another space and time dimension in my head when the lectures start.

But you can't tell people stories like this, because then they will worry, or call home to see if you are all right, and then there will only be *more rage*.

At me. Or in the air. Rage *like* air, present but

invisible, permeating everything. Taking up the space behind my eyes that is not otherwise occupied by the tight, prickly feeling of wanting to cry.

There is *outside the house,* and *inside the house,* and what is spoken of outside is not welcome inside, and vice versa. They are two spheres that must never meet, orbiting politely at a distance. With me in the middle, caught in the heavy gravity, slowly tearing apart.

Actually, more even than the rage, maybe what I mostly feel is *the fear.*

Not just mine. Which is always present, like a low-level background hum that only I can hear, ready to ramp up in a heartbeat. I'm constantly afraid of setting off all the little bombs I don't even know I've trodden on until they go off in my face. *Was it something I said? Was it the missing 48 per cent on my maths quiz? Was it because I asked for more cafeteria money? What?*

But there is also always *his* fear. The fear of people being rude to him because he *speaks funny,* of people not giving him the respect he deserves because even though he manages a Chinese restaurant now, he was once a promising young doctor in China who couldn't get into a specialist medical college here, even though he tried four times.

The last time he failed the exam, when I was ten, Dad went missing for hours, and my mother burst into tears the minute she heard his key in the door, at 3:12 the next morning. I know that because the sound woke me up, and the numbers on my alarm clock seemed to grow redder and brighter as she cried, and he yelled.

Lots of things changed after that time, the fourth time. Things seemed even less possible than before.

"I am forced," Dad shouted once, "to be nice to drunk people who are too stupid to understand that the hot, rolled, steamed cloth napkin that I bring them at the end of the meal is not for eating, but for wiping their faces and hands with!"

Dad is wary of policemen, parking inspectors, council workers, people who aren't like us. He speaks four Chinese languages fluently, Mom always tells me in a low voice, he loves classical Chinese poetry and can play two instruments to concert standard, *but none of it is good enough in this country.* I've never seen any of this. We don't have music on in the house, just SBS Mandarin, and I never see anybody read. If Dad loves all that, it's locked inside his head somewhere.

I think Dad's problem is that he's too proud. He's given up on being the surgeon he always wanted to be because he refuses to sit the exams ever again. He can't ever take criticism, and he can't ever yield. There is no other side, except his side. Always.

Even without passing the specialist exams, Dad could work in the emergency department of any hospital tomorrow. They really need people like him—with perfect recall, steady hands and an unflappable demeanor. But he won't do that. It's not good enough. It's too far short of the dreams that he had for himself. So he's cut and burned that whole part of himself off, years and years of studying and training and dreaming, which is why he is now the angriest, most ruthless floor manager of the Hai Tong Tai Seafood Restaurant in history.

He often spits, "They are missing out!"

Meaning all the hospitals in this country and, possibly, everywhere else in the world.

But I think *he's* missing out. Because he won't *try* anymore. One life, this life, that's it, finished and done and over.

Which explains why, sometimes, my dad doesn't get out of bed for days, and only goes back to work at the restaurant when they call Mom to say they're giving him the sack, and she is forced to plead on the phone, in rapid, desperate Cantonese, for his job. My mom, who wouldn't usually say *boo* to a goose yet can speak four languages herself, though she only uses one of them at home and another one at the Chinese grocery shop near our house, in a voice barely louder than a whisper.

Mom knows all about *the fear*. She gave up everything when she married Dad—parties with friends, random, spontaneous outings, her university degree, her country, her parents, her sisters and brothers, the latest fashions, *fun*—and I know that being with him has made her smaller. I can tell when I look at the one photo album she brought with her to this country that she used to be a different person. She was decisive, I know she was. She was groovy. She was *young*.

Now, too many choices on a Chinese restaurant menu will confuse her so badly that she'll grow red in the face, her voice dwindling to a whisper, and leave it to Dad to order for all of us. She will always defer. She will always give way.

And he never let her learn how to drive when we got here, so she never learned to read a map and has to walk everywhere.

We have to walk everywhere.

If Mom runs out of household money for the month—for food, for public transport—she's too afraid to ask for more because *the trouble,* and he gives her plenty, *isn't worth it*. She's been conditioned not to speak up, not to decide; just to exist, just to support.

She's like an anxious, hovering shadow. Not expecting much, not entitled to much.

I sometimes catch her standing in front of her diminishing wardrobe of jewel-bright, ladylike skirt suits that she brought with her from China over a decade ago. I can tell from her face if she's fretting about whether the almost invisible darns are showing or agonizing over whether to throw something away because it's gone beyond saving. Like me, she wouldn't dream of asking Dad for any clothes money, because it will set him off; he's like a walking lecture machine, and she knows he wouldn't hand it over anyway.

You're not a doctor's wife anymore. So there's no point. That's what Dad would say with his perfect, icy logic. So Mom mends, she makes do, she dwindles.

Mom's whole life has our small house—that smells faintly of mold and is always chilly and shrouded in stain-resistant plastic hall runners and furniture covers—at the dead centre of it. I know she had one job really, to have a son, and she managed to stuff even that up. I heard Dad shout that once, through their bedroom door, followed by the words *failure* and *disappointment.*

So Mom and Dad are a package deal. If he says *No,* Mom's *Maybe, yes?* becomes a *No* too. She's expected to have a big bowl of soup for us to share, plus at least seven more dishes as well as rice, on the table on the days that Dad isn't working at the restaurant—eight dishes for luck, or there will be problems, no answering back. She's also expected to iron all the tablecloths and napkins he brings home from the restaurant for her to wash, keep the house tidy, get the best discounts on fresh meat, fruit and vegetables at the market or the grocery store, get me to and from school on foot *(No stops!)* and have her hair and makeup perfect every day after she gets out of bed. And those are the very outer limits of her life.

I imagine our footsteps, Mom's and mine, carving these narrow lines into the path between home and school, between the local shops and home, without deviation; every day getting a little deeper. She actually doesn't walk everywhere, she scurries, as if someone has a stopwatch on her. That's the only way I can describe it. Mom's life is a beep test. A beep test without end.

You're lucky to have this, to even be here in this country! Dad reminds Mom constantly. *Because you were already old for an unmarried woman, and no good at your studies.*

No brain, no application, no prospects.

I know that's what Dad thinks I'm like too, because he constantly calls me *lazy, stupid, small* and *insolent* and says that I watch too much television and will end up being *nothing.*

I don't care so much about the birthday parties or

the sleepovers. I don't care that I find out a lot later about things that friends have gone to that I was never invited to because most people have given up asking.

When the answer is always *No*, people get the wrong idea about you: that you're not interested, or just too difficult. A princess (even if you're as opposite to a real princess as it's possible to be). Or they think you just don't like them. I get that.

Well, *I do* care. But I have a plan.

Because unlike my mom, one day I will be free. And even though I'm *lazy, stupid, small* and *insolent* and watch too much TV, my friend Henry is going to help me get there.

CHAPTER 2

BAD NEWS HAS WINGS

BECAUSE I'M NO GOOD AT MATHS, AND LOVE reading, long-distance running, dancing and drawing, Dad has pretty much given up on me and tells me all the time that I'm destined to be a waitress, like that's a bad thing, or a housewife like my mother if I'm lucky.

No amount of extra maths tuition on Saturday mornings or extra helpings of maths homework have been able to sew shut the maths-shaped gap in my brain. I'm *impervious* to *improvement,* I tell Henry, loftily, all the time. That's a fancy way of saying I am resistant to mathematical theory in any shape or form.

You do not take after me! Dad roars every time I bring another maths test home with all the letters of the alphabet on it, except the one that really matters.

She takes after me, Mom will murmur tiredly. *I was not very strong in maths.*

To which Dad will give his usual response in Chinese, *Useless.*

Or *No brain.*

But my study buddy, Henry, is more stubborn than I am and keeps telling me, *You're getting better all the time.* He's made it his mission to get me to an A in maths the way I'm trying to get him to an A in English. Henry's always complaining that English, the language and/or the subject, makes no sense, especially the writing of stories, and that nothing is sufficiently certain. I tell him it's the opposite for me with maths—it's all too sufficiently certain and there's no room for improvisation, which is what I am good at. I tell him English is like drawing, more free-flowing and imaginative, which Henry is good at too, although he doesn't think so. But Henry's pictures are like his maths—precise and detailed and internally consistent. He doesn't think drawing is important to life on earth, the way I do.

Henry's family came from a different part of China than we did, and only arrived a year ago, so when he speaks he's almost impossible to understand; that's what all the other kids say. But we're the only two Chinese kids in our class, so at first, he had to hang with me for necessity, and now we're actually mates. When people want to talk to Henry, or vice versa, they have to go through me.

He's like a kid behind glass, kind of untouchable and remote. He won't let anyone but me get too close, because he's already hurrying on his way to somewhere else—somewhere better. And that's the beauty of being Henry's friend. Because when it all gets to be too much, and too hard, especially at home, he reminds me that one day things will change for both of us. They have to.

"We're comets," he will say simply. "We're going to burn our way out of here and leave a trail that people can see."

My usual response to that? "Sure, keep believing that, mate."

But, still, it would be amazing if it came true.

Henry's dad, who left school at fifteen in China, works for a distant relative at the fresh fruit and vegetable markets near where we live. He gets up before dawn every morning, leaving Henry's much younger mother—who can't speak any English at all—at home all day by herself. Henry gets himself to and from school while his mom watches Chinese-language TV and cries.

Mom says it's widely known, and talked about, what a *bad mother* Fay Xiao is. Often when Henry's dad gets home from the market, late in the afternoon, Henry's mom won't have moved at all from where she's been sitting in her armchair opposite the TV. The house will be dark and cold, and there will be no food on the table or in the fridge. On the very worst days, when she's paralyzed by sadness, she won't even have washed her face or brushed her hair. Henry says when his mom isn't crying, she's screaming at his dad, who is like this tense, angry knot all the time.

"The house is either silent, or on fire," Henry tells me, half in Mandarin and half in English, which I insist that he use so that he can practice.

"Since you're stuck here, like I am," I remind him casually, "you might as well try to speak English."

And Henry will screw up his face and end up making both of us laugh helplessly with the twisted words that come out of his mouth. "Rs are kind of optional in Chinese, remember?" he snorts as we laugh at each other in a way that Mr. Cornish's before-school English class has no right to do.

"Stand in my shoes, be inside my skin," Henry once said grimly, "and then you may laugh."

I tell Henry about my dad all the time, all the things he does, and Henry completely gets it—how fury is like this thing that holds the entire house up; how all of us are suspended like hot-air balloons and drifting further and further away from each other, and from our true selves. Henry understands how anger has tides and temperatures and speeds that can suck you down or spit you out, depending on the day, the hour, the moment—changing you forever.

"Who knows what would happen if, suddenly, all that anger disappeared?" Henry said once. "What would we do with ourselves then?"

"We would feel joy," I'd replied immediately, sure of it. "Life wouldn't seem so . . . narrow."

"Yes," Henry had replied simply, understanding right away.

Henry wants an A in English to match all the other ones he gets for science, maths, IT and design and technology. One day, he wants to build airplanes from the ground up, from wheels to seat covers. He is obsessed with flying, with machines, with speed and power, with speaking the international language of numbers so that he will never feel tongue-tied again and can talk to anyone, from any country, in numbers and pictures and fiendish 3D diagrams.

His plan is to escape his awful home life by going for a place at that big high school that's so far away from home—near some huge mansions by the sea—that it could be on another planet. Just about everything will be solved, Henry says, if he can get that place at that school full of clever kids. And Miss Spencer is in on Henry's plan as well. That's who Henry got his idea from—the idea that people who come out of that selective school by the sea can do anything, and be anything. It gives him the feeling of *infinite possibility*. And that feeling, of being able to do anything, or be anything, is very much missing from Henry's life. So the mere idea of that school, and going to that school—even if it will take him two separate bus lines to get there, over an hour on the road each way, or four hours of extra study at night—is something so powerful, it gets him out of bed when he doesn't want to.

Against my better judgment, Henry's convinced me to sit the entrance exam as well. That's our project for *me*, even though I still think of it as largely theoretical and almost wholly fantastical. He says if the school sees one of the stories I write, and the way that I draw, how hard and how far I can run, they will want me to go there too. Mostly, I think Henry's dreaming—how could a school like that want someone who can't even do long division properly?—but a small part of me is excited that I might have a chance at a different life too. Just a small part.

The part of me that isn't sensible or realistic.

Miss Spencer and Henry put in all the forms for me. The forms claimed that I live at Henry's home address, and I'd asked, shocked, "But what about my parents? They would never say *yes* to this."

Miss Spencer's mouth had gone all tight and funny and she'd said, "We'll deal with that hurdle when we come to it, Wen."

When I reach the classroom on Tuesday morning, Henry isn't in his usual seat in the corner, up the back. I don't bother asking Nikki or Michaela where he is, because most people don't talk to him; in fact, they seem a little afraid to.

In the beginning they tried, and some kids—the jokers and the mean ones—even stole his phone out of his hands when he was looking at it and held it away from him for hours, or shoved him around or tripped him up, just for a laugh. But people leave him alone now because there is something so wise, and sad, and clearly *special* about Henry. He always knows the answer—any class, any subject, any question. If you're a kid who can't even speak properly but can't ever be caught out, that means something around here. People just let him be these days, because he looks like, any moment, he could break apart.

Miss Spencer's up the front, glancing with a frown at Henry's empty seat and taking the roll, when the deputy principal, bosomy blonde-tipped Mrs. Douglas-Williams, hurries into the classroom and whispers in her ear. Miss Spencer actually drops her clipboard, which falls to the ground with a *bang* like a gun going off.

We all jump, muttering among ourselves when Miss Spencer leaves the room with Mrs. Douglas-Williams, a hand over her mouth, and doesn't come back at all for the rest of the day.

Mr. Fraser, the geography teacher, who's really bad with kids, takes over. You can tell he hates kids, and wishes he were something else, like an international airline pilot, or a spy. And we wonder what could have happened to Miss Spencer to make her just leave like that. She loves us, and she loves teaching, the way Mr. Fraser doesn't, you can tell.

We all forgot about Henry, completely. Even me.

The next day, Henry's still not in his chair and I'm the only one who knows that yesterday and today are connected, because while all the other kids are laboriously writing a narrative—which I've already finished, because I could write stories all day, it's not even work, honestly—Miss Spencer takes me aside in the tiny staff kitchen next door to our classroom.

"It's about Henry," she says, blinking rapidly, and something inside me switches to high alert immediately. "I know how close you are . . ." And I'm horrified when her big brown eyes become shiny. I go hot, then cold, thinking of all the things that might have happened to Henry. Like, did he have an *accident*?

I relax a little when she says, "You need to convince him to come back to school. It's really, really important. The entrance exam is in less than two weeks. The finish line is right there. You're almost *there*, the two of you. You've worked so hard."

"Has he got cold feet?" I ask, wrinkling my nose in consternation. "I can't do it without him. We were supposed to do this together. I can't believe he's thinking of quitting! That's so *selfish*."

As soon as I say the word *selfish*, Miss Spencer places both her hands on my shoulders and closes her eyes tightly, drawing a deep breath. I'm horrified all over again when I see that her mouth is . . . *quivering*. When she opens her eyes, there are tears in them. I don't know what to do—should I just pat her shoulder? Find her a tissue? Call for help?

As I'm panicking about what to do, Miss Spencer finally lets go of me, crossing her arms and stepping back. She's wearing black trousers and a white shirt today and looks like a sad panda with a cloud of brown hair around her small, heart-shaped face. I don't know what to say and neither does she, because I can almost see her picking the words she's going to use, in her head; examining each one and dropping some of them in favor of others. She's silent for a long time.

Her voice is funny, but her words, when she finally speaks, are very careful. "I don't know . . . if you know Henry's mother, Fay?"

I shake my head, confused about how Henry's mother—his silent, ghostlike mother, who refuses to do any actual mothering and is staging a sit-in protest about her own life—could have any impact on Henry's decision not to do the exam. Once Henry decides to do something, that's it, it's done. Or as good as. There is this part of him that's made of actual iron.

"Doesn't she want him to go ahead with it?" I ask in a small voice, and I'm worried about me, I admit. I can't do it by myself. It was *our* plan, not just mine. I'm not brave enough. I'm only sharing Henry's dream. The dream was too big for me in the first place.

Miss Spencer makes a weird, hiccupping noise and shakes her head so that her tight curls and big gold earrings bounce around. "I don't think Mrs. Xiao even knew what Henry was planning. She had nothing to do with it . . ." Her mouth starts turning down again at the corners.

I step back in alarm, trying to put some distance between me and her.

". . . and *everything* to do with it." Miss Spencer suddenly looks down at her shoes, her shoulders shaking.

I'm used to my dad telling me *No* to everything; how final and hopeless and immovable that feels. "Did she tell him *No*?" I ask tentatively as Miss Spencer rubs the heel of one hand across her eyes. "Do you want me to explain how important the entrance exam is to Henry's mom? Do you want me to change her mind? I can speak to her," I add eagerly. "She'll understand me. We share a common dialect, the same way Henry and I do. I can go over there and talk to her."

Miss Spencer finally sweeps her wet, smudgy brown eyes back up to mine, and says in a low voice, "Wen, I don't know how to tell you this, but Henry's mom . . . she died yesterday. Henry was getting ready for school and found her in their backyard. By the time he got outside there wasn't anything he could do. His dad had already been gone for hours. We only know because the police called us and I went over to check on him and there he was . . ."

There's suddenly no air in the room, and I start shaking too.

". . . trying to *deal* with it." A tear slides down Miss Spencer's cheek, and we both pretend it isn't there.

"I'm really afraid"—she pulls herself together with difficulty, the words forming on her lips even though I'm unable to make sense of them through the roaring in my ears—"for Henry. He needs to come back from this. He can't be allowed to give up, not now. We have to do everything we can to help him."

In art class in the afternoon, the boys give me a hard time for the entire period. But I just ignore them. I have to finish my work, and Henry has to understand what it means. Fatima gives my arm a quick squeeze of encouragement as she passes to get more sequins and glue, but like most of my other friends, doesn't know what to say. Someone in the principal's office must have blabbed after they hung up on the police and what's happened to Henry's mom is everywhere, everyone knows already, it's the worst thing anyone can possibly imagine, you wouldn't wish it on your worst enemy.

"Ooooooh," some of the boys say. "Wen's got the hots for Henry. Just look at what she's making him!"

I know it's over the top. I can't help it. I'm trying

to tell Henry how important he is, this is, how important our plan is for the both of us. How dreams, just like food, can keep you alive. I'm trying to tell him that someone cares. Not just in words, but in cardboard and paper, plastic beads and glitter glue. As vital as words are, sometimes they aren't enough.

After school, Mom is waiting for me as usual, her long, sleek black hair tucked behind her ears. She's wearing a neat pink skirt suit and white blouse, her white handbag slung over one arm in exactly the same shade of white as her high-heeled shoes. Pearl earrings. Immaculate, just the way Dad likes her to dress, even when he can't see her, even though he won't give her money for any new clothes. She represents him, you see, at all times. Which means she never wears jeans or gym gear or sandals. She doesn't even own any.

She looks very pretty. If you don't look too closely, you can't see that her suit is fading around the neckline and armpits, and that she's had to stitch up the right pocket of her blazer so that it doesn't hang lower than the other pocket. On the surface, she's shipshape and spick-and-span.

I don't have time to explain to Mom what I'm doing, I just run all the way to Henry's house, which we have passed almost every day of our lives since we arrived in this country. It's on the main road, almost in the shadow of a huge concrete pedestrian bridge that goes over the top of the traffic to get from my side of the suburb to Henry's side. They say over fifty thousand cars travel past his house every day. I don't even know how he can study for the honking, the fumes and the noise from all the cars and long-distance trucks that speed by on their way to somewhere else, somewhere distant.

Trailing behind, protesting, Mom does what she always does. She follows.

When I stop outside Henry's place, my heart is hammering and sweat is running down my back, under my school sweatshirt, between my shoulder blades.

When Mom demands in Chinese what we're doing here, why I made her run in her *only pair of good shoes left,* I tell her to be quiet, because this is important. Her mouth snaps shut in outrage. I know I will pay for this insolence later somehow, because Mom tells Dad about everything that I do, right or wrong. Mostly wrong, because after Dad hears about my latest misdeed, or failure of judgment, he will usually quote something obscure from the philosopher Confucius like *There are young plants that fail to produce blossoms, and blossoms that fail to produce fruit,* and my parents will frown at me, together, in the certainty that my future is likely to be blossomless, or fruitless, if I continue in the disastrous way that I'm going.

I study the front of Henry's house while Mom fumes beside me, every hair, and her foofy white blouse, still immaculate, while I'm puffing and red-faced and sweaty.

As always, the curtains in the window that looks out onto the tiny, patchy front yard are tightly drawn and there are weeds everywhere, in all the beds, because weeds are the least of anyone's concerns, in the Xiao household. I know Henry's bedroom is down the back, right beside the laundry. It looks onto the twisted apple tree, which is almost the only living thing in the Xiaos' entire backyard. He told me that. He said even the grass had given up, and that they don't grow grass back there, they grow mushrooms and snails.

Nothing survives but that tree.

I can't imagine what Henry saw, or felt, when he woke to go to school two days ago. What did he do? What would I have done, if it were my mother I saw through the window? I go cold inside, even though my pretty mother, dressed all in white and pink like a neat gift, is standing right here, anger and incomprehension and fear rising and rising under her skin like blood.

I ring the doorbell and hear nothing. No footsteps, no noises. Maybe no one is home. But I know Henry must be home. In his tiny, peeling bedroom filled with Chinese books and English books that would tell anyone who is paying attention that he is a boy on a mission to get up and out of here, the street of fifty thousand cars and trucks. I ring the doorbell again and again.

In the front window of the small, single-story house next door, built in exactly the same style as Henry's but with added black mold growing up the striped awning that hangs over it, I see a curtain twitch, and know that someone is watching me and my hovering, overdressed mother. That Henry's horrible, nosy old neighbor, who yells *Ching chong Chinaman!* over the side fence at Henry's family whenever he hears any of them moving around the garden, might even rush out and tell us, in awful detail that I don't want to know, what happened to Fay Xiao.

What she did to herself, *the silly cow*.

With Mom now hissing at me ("Your father told us no stops, Wen! No stops! Is this not a stop?") I crouch hurriedly at the base of the steel security door and fumble the thing that I made in art class out of my backpack, feeding it under the door. I make sure the lavish confection of cardboard and paper, beads and glue, disappears entirely through the gap so that it's safely inside Henry's house. Where he might find it before it's too late.

I made it this shape because I don't want him to lose heart. It's as simple and corny as that.

Inside the card, all I wrote, because today I had no words to describe what I was feeling, was:

You're not going anywhere without me.
And I'm not doing this without you.

As I crouch there, listening at the door for a little too long, Mom surges forward and wrenches me up by the arm onto my feet. And this time it's Mom running home in her good shoes, dragging me all the way, *the fear* hanging over both of us.

CHAPTER 3

NOT DO, NOT DIE

Bù zuò, bù sǐ

WHEN WE GET HOME, THE LANDLINE IS ALREADY ringing. Dad is checking, like he always does, that everything is in its place in our little world, and that I'm doing my homework and not *snacking to the point where you get fat.*

I'm still out of breath, and my forearm hurts from where it was clenched in Mom's apprehensive claw the whole way home. I shake my head when she gestures at me with the handset. I can't speak to him today; he'll be able to tell from my voice that something is very wrong. I'll have no answers to the inevitable questions about school, the icy sarcasm, the reminders of my many and various failings. I'm not in the mood to be picked on, or compared to unproductive trees today.

Mom doesn't tell Dad about the detour because she still doesn't understand why we were standing outside *that woman's* badly kept house on the main road. She says this immediately after she hangs up on the sounds of the cooking and wait staff at the Hai Tong Tai Seafood Restaurant stuffing down a quick early dinner before the dinner rush begins.

"Why were you sending . . ." Her eyes widen at the memory of the heart-shaped thing I shoved under the front door. ". . . *notes* to the Xiao boy? Is he your boyfriend?" At the words *boy* and *friend*, in rapid Mandarin, Mom's voice rises, panicked. "No boyfriend!" she insists. "Too young for boyfriend! What will I tell your father?"

I can't stop my face crumpling as I reply in the same language, "Henry de māmā, zìshā."

Henry's mom killed herself.

There is no way to dress up words like that. They are as blunt and final as they sound.

And they sound so wrong in my mouth that I can't help crying, just like Miss Spencer did.

Mom freezes where she's standing and inhales sharply, as if she's drowning and going under a wave, the exact same way I did on our last school excursion to Cape Schanck to look at an old lighthouse and a bunch of rockpools. I lost my footing on the rocks and had to be saved out of a riptide by a student teacher, who ended up with stitches trying to protect me from getting smashed. All I can remember is going under and going under and going under until it seemed that all the water was in me and through me; there was no beginning or end to the water. I couldn't reach the light, for all the weight of the water above me, and I was so far out, by the end, that I was flotsam. It was the closest I've ever come to just giving up.

Mom's eyes are very bright as she puts one hand over her mouth, briefly, then leans against the kitchen bench for support.

She doesn't try to touch me as I cry, or come any closer. There are a thousand expressions flitting across her face as she watches me silently, and I think she's actually going to say something else when she murmurs instead, "Bù zuò, bù sǐ."

It's my turn to inhale sharply.

The words mean *Not do, not die.* What she said was: it was Henry's mom's *fault* for doing something stupid that led to this tragedy. Action, consequence.

Fay Xiao should have known better.

"How can you say that?" I reply, shocked, in English. "Henry's mom *died* and that's all you can say?"

"To show weakness like that is . . . *unfixable*," Mom replies fiercely in Chinese, almost hissing in distress. "If every woman did that in a moment of, of . . . weakness, of pain, the world—it would be full of motherless children! I *abhor* her actions. She has cursed herself, and her son. She has marked him forever. Can't you see that?"

"She was *sad*," I shout. "She was sad enough to kill herself, Mom."

"We are all sad, Wen," Mom says, tiredly. "Some of us just hide it better. Now go and shower." She turns away and takes off her immaculate pink jacket before strapping on a black apron and knotting up her shiny hair in a low, rough ponytail. "Do your homework, especially your maths. It's the only way to get better at it. Do it until he has no more words to say on the matter because words will no longer be necessary. Dinner is in twenty minutes, no arguments."

When I think of my dad and my mom, I actually think of two different philosophies of life, two "Ways" of being, if you like.

Dad, in my head, is always this famous Chinese philosopher called Confucius, who said helpful things like *Being good as a son and obedient as a young man is, perhaps, the root of a man's character*, and Mom is this other famous Chinese philosopher called Lao Tzu, who would have replied (more calmly than perhaps he was feeling, if he were arguing with someone as infuriating and inflexible as my father):

Know contentment
And you will suffer no disgrace;
Know when to stop
And you will meet with no danger.
You can then endure.

You can tell which Way makes more sense to me, because I'm not a son, and I'm not a man, not even a young one, not now, not ever. Confucius, I always think, when Dad hits me with another round of ancient philosophical wisdom, or just with whatever is handy in warning against talking back, is a fish bicycle to most Chinese girls. His Way has no room for us in it anywhere, and I have to suppress an acute eye-roll every time I hear a quote about what a *gentleman* or *scholar* would do in similar circumstances, or the shortcomings of *small men*.

Not my actual, specific problem, Dad, I always think. *No men in this house but you. Small or otherwise.*

I'm reminded of all this the minute Dad gets home, near midnight as usual. He always makes a huge racket coming into the house, because he can; he's worked hard all day, and he's tired, and he wants Mom (and me) to know exactly how tired he is, how very late the hour. I haven't been able to sleep anyway, wondering what Henry and his dad are doing right now, in that cold, unwelcoming house.

I hear Mom tell Dad hurriedly about Henry's mom's suicide before Dad's even had time to hang up his overcoat. And Dad uses that actual word, *disgrace*, after a moment of shocked silence, and then says dismissively, "Fay Xiao was weak, that much was well-known. She did not conduct herself properly while she was alive, and now she has brought Ah Yuan and his connections great shame. We must all learn from this."

I lie there in the dark, unable to sleep after Mom and Dad move away down the hall towards the kitchen, burning with the great unfeelingness of him, how the biggest crisis in Henry's life has been reduced to a teaching moment—a veiled warning to my mother to *endure,* or else.

On the way to school in the morning, Mom picks up her pace in her tan high heels as we pass Henry's house, which looks as closed and blank as ever.

As she drags at my arm, hissing, "Hurry, you'll be late," her head turned sharply away from the Xiao house so as not to have to look at it, or consider what's going on beyond its bland, blond-brick façade, I see a man's hand draw the closed curtains in the front windows even more tightly shut. I crane my neck back in wonder that Henry's dad is actually home, during the day.

Because Mr. Xiao brings the fresh stock back from the wholesale fruit and vegetable sellers in a rusty truck before the local market opens, then hauls things like huge bunches of bananas all day, he has to get up every morning before it's light (except Mondays), re-turning around four in the afternoon to see to Henry's dinner. My dad is usually at home in bed until at least ten in the morning because he *works like a dog until late* and doesn't leave home for work until just after eleven.

Dad's and Mr. Xiao's paths should never cross, but the Chinese community here revolves around the local market and the local shops, and I wonder how Mr. Xiao can bear everyone *knowing*. When we stopped (very quickly) at the pharmacy for more Band-Aids for my eczema, even the pharmacist, Mrs. Xenakis, wanted to have a chat about the Xiao family and asked if she could do anything to help *that poor boy and his father*.

When we reach school, and Mom has tottered away in her impractical shoes, matching tan bag and neat mauve skirt suit with discreet repairs to the lining under the armpits that no one ever sees except me, Miss Spencer catches me at the lockers before she goes in to mark the class roll. In her hand is a plain manila envelope stuffed so full of papers that it can't be sealed properly. She has a thinner one for me, with my name on it.

"Henry's not here again," she says hurriedly. "When I called his house this morning, his father said he wasn't feeling well, and I didn't want to push it. I know you go past his place on your way home—Henry's told me that before. Can you leave him these? We can't let things slip. It's too important—especially now. It's revision. You've got the benefit of me talking at you all day, Wen, but he doesn't."

I have to remember to shut my mouth after Miss Spencer walks away, and put the envelope for Henry into the mesh side pocket of my backpack so that seeing it facing out all day will remind me about what I have to do. We're going to have to make a stop on the way home whether Mom likes it or not.

"Not again," Mom says in Mandarin as I halt outside the Xiao house. "*No.* There's nothing we can do. We shouldn't get involved. Your father, *his* father, wouldn't want that!"

I give Mom such a fierce look that she drops her hand from my elbow as if she's been scalded. I swing my backpack off my shoulder and place it on the ground, crouching to pull the rolled-up envelope of papers Miss Spencer gave me out of the side pocket. Before I think too hard about what I'm doing, I march to the door and press the doorbell three times.

Henry will speak to me, I'm sure of it.

There's a long silence before I hear the shuffle of slippers approaching the front door. There's the sound of a chain being pushed across and the wooden door finally opens, but I can't see who's standing there because the heavy wire security door is impossible to see through in the bright afternoon sunlight—I can only make out a vague dark shape. I say politely in Chinese, "Miss Spencer, the teacher, she wants Henry to do this homework. It's very important."

If it's Henry, or even his dad, mentioning Miss Spencer will get their attention.

But the dark shape says nothing, and begins to close the front door. "Wait! Please!" I say, but the door clicks shut and I'm still standing there, holding the envelope.

From behind me, Mom says firmly, "Henry is his

father's responsibility, not ours. You are *embarrassing* them. It is not our business. Let them grieve in peace."

Ignoring her, I pull a pen out of the pocket of my tracksuit pants and scribble a maths problem and answer onto the envelope, not even deliberately mucking up the answer because I still don't *get* long division. Just about all the numbers are in the wrong columns.

$$8\overline{)629} \quad \tfrac{7 \quad 8}{}$$

$$\begin{array}{r} 7\ \ 8 \\ 8\overline{)629} \\ 5\,6 \\ \hline 6\,9 \\ 6\,4 \\ \hline 5 \\ = 78 \end{array}$$

I say fiercely, "If that doesn't get your attention, Henry Xiao, nothing will." Then I bend and stuff the envelope through the gap under the wire door and it's so overfull that it tears a little as I keep shoving it through under the wooden door behind until nothing can be seen from the outside.

Mom has to take little running steps all the way home to keep up with me.

"What are you *doing?*" Mom exclaims as I get a colorful plastic lunchbox out of the bottom drawer beneath the cutlery drawer and the tea towel drawer and bring it to the table. Our simple dinner of a whole steamed fish, rice and beans fried with a little minced pork and pickled vegetables is sitting on it. I shovel rice, a handful of fried beans and a long piece of fish from near the spine into the box, and shut it tight.

"As soon as we eat, I'm taking it to Henry's," I reply firmly. "I bet he's not even eating. I couldn't smell any food being cooked when I was at the door before."

"That's enough!" Mom snaps, snatching up the lunchbox and ripping off the lid before tipping the food into the empty bowl in front of me. "There's only enough food here for *two* people. It's terrible what happened to that . . . what that woman did, but it's not up to us to raise her son when she couldn't do that herself! *It's not our business.* She obviously wasn't properly taught. Now, it's a great shame, but her son will not be either. And you're not taking food out of your mouth to put into his! *He's not one of our people.*"

As calmly as I can, I pull the lunchbox back towards me and dump the uneaten contents of my bowl into it again and close the lid, placing the box on the seat beside me so that Mom can't reach it. I pick up my chopsticks and start serving my mother some of the remaining beans and fish while she stares at me in disbelief.

"He is my good friend," I reply quietly in Chinese, "and he still needs to eat. If it had happened to me"— Mom inhales loudly at the highly unlucky suggestion, unluckily spoken aloud—"you would want me to be taken care of because Dad would not be capable, he would not be willing. You know this. How many times have you heard him say *Raising children is not a job for a man!* It's the least we can do. Henry can't study if he's hungry."

I don't remind Mom how often Confucius himself banged on about how important it was to be a *benevolent man,* because I can see how stricken she is at my words. There is not much time for benevolence in our house, but now is one such time. Underneath *the fear,* Mom's a good person. She's kind, and softly spoken, and so very desperate to please. Without *the fear,* I know she would be a different person, a braver one. She might even have already cooked the Xiaos a proper meal and taken it over herself on a tray, while it was still hot. But she's been conditioned to stay in her box, so she does. She can't see over the sides of it, wouldn't even think of testing its edges and dimensions, and it's both sad and terrifying to me.

We don't really talk as we put on our coats after cleaning up the dinner dishes. Mom trails behind me, looking around anxiously as if Dad might somehow pop out of the bushes, roaring and pointing accusingly, as I walk back to Henry's house holding the lunchbox balanced across my palms like an offering.

When we reach the Xiaos' place, the whole house is as dark as the night outside. If they are in there, they're at the very back of the house, or they're pretending to be asleep in their separate, tiny bedrooms. When I ring the doorbell, three times firmly with a decent pause between each ring, no one comes to the door, and no lights turn on.

"Wen," Mom says quietly, "just leave it now."

When Dad gets home that night, near midnight, like always when he's working, I listen hard to what they say to each other, but Mom doesn't mention stopping at Henry's house at all.

And I think, *It's a step.*

CHAPTER 4

COMMON PEOPLE

IN THE MORNING, ON THE WAY TO SCHOOL, EVEN
Mom is looking out anxiously for Henry's house. I
can feel her tension through her hand on my elbow
as we cross the concrete pedestrian bridge to Henry's
side of the road, the traffic already slow and heavy beneath us.

"Look," she says in Chinese, "it's there. And the
papers."

We both rush forward to retrieve the things on the
front doorstep; the envelope with the lunchbox neatly
placed on top, everything at perfect right angles. Mom
lifts the box, opening it to find that it's empty, and
sniffs at it. We both catch the faint smell of fake lemons from the water it's been washed in. "Do you think

Henry ate it?" she says cautiously. "Or did he just throw it away? It looked terrible, the food we gave him. Not even like food."

"That was your fault," I mutter. "At least it *looked* like food when I first put it in the box!"

I peer into the torn envelope still stuffed full of papers and draw one of the worksheets out. I didn't realize I was holding my breath until I let it out now with a *whoosh*. It's a maths worksheet covered in Henry's precise script—lines and lines of working-out. Rifling through the remaining papers in the envelope, I also see Henry's responses to short-answer English comprehension questions, to multiple-choice science questions, pages and pages of work.

I don't think Miss Spencer expected him to do all this stuff *in one night*, but Henry has. Maybe he didn't even sleep. Maybe he couldn't, and this helped him to pass the time.

Seeing this, Mom murmurs, "Poor boy," and we keep walking towards school, Mom holding the empty lunchbox and me holding the papers. Before she leaves me at the gate, Mom says tentatively, "I think I'll make a healthy soup tonight. With gǒu qǐ, lotus root, carrots, mushrooms, dried longan, chicken."

I can't help the smile that breaks across my face. "Could you just make more?" I reply. "Make lots?"

Sounding distracted, Mom isn't really speaking to me as she turns away, muttering, "And noodles. Something hearty and good for the mind, the eyes, the circulation. To relieve the stress."

I catch Miss Spencer just before we both walk into the classroom and hand her the torn envelope. "He did *all* of it," I tell her quietly, and Miss Spencer's eyes widen in amazement.

Billy Raum notices us talking on his way to his seat at the back of the classroom. He mouths *swot* in my direction, and I give him my best murderous look out of my slant-eyes-that-don't-slant that says, *So what if I am?*

Billy's eyes widen too, and he looks down.

Miss Spencer's eyebrows almost touch her hairline as she takes the papers out, sifting through them quickly. "Can you take him more worksheets after school?" she replies, sounding just as distracted as Mom was at the school gates. "I called again—Henry's dad says he's refusing to leave home, to even step outside his bedroom. Won't go with his dad to the market, won't talk to him, or to anyone else. And put this in the bin," she says, handing me the ripped envelope she's holding. "It's wrecked."

"I couldn't fit it under the door," I say apologetically. Miss Spencer's smile is a bit sad. "But *never say die*, right, Wen? Keep pushing till you can push no more— that's the way. I'll find another envelope to put the new batch in. And I won't give him as much work or he'll kill himself . . ." We look at each other quickly, horrified, before Miss Spencer adds, ". . . trying to do it all in one day. See you inside."

She continues flicking through Henry's sheaf of completed worksheets in wonder as I take the torn envelope towards the recycling bin at the back. "There's a note on the front, Wen," Nikki Kuol points out helpfully as I pass her desk, "in red." And I see that Henry has painstakingly corrected the long division maths problem I hastily scribbled on the envelope before I shoved it under the door. He's moved all the numbers into the correct columns and highlighted the number I didn't know what to do with and just left hanging there.

Nikki and I both laugh as we read the outraged message printed neatly in capitals across the bottom.

"I do that too, all the time," Nikki says ruefully as I post the envelope through the slot on the bin lid.

$$
\begin{array}{r}
7\!\!\!\nearrow\ 8 \\
8\overline{)629} \\
56 \\
\overline{69} \longrightarrow \\
64 \longrightarrow \\
\overline{5} \longrightarrow \\
=78\ r\ 5
\end{array}
$$

YOU FORGOT THE
REMAINDER!

Just before art class, the last period of the day, Miss Spencer hands me a new envelope for Henry as she passes me in the hallway. "I've already put yours on your desk," she adds. "Remember to take it home with you. Just don't, whatever you do, forget to drop this work to Henry. If he's happy to communicate with the world this way, and *only* this way, I'll take it."

During art class, instead of working on my design for a convict ship like I'm supposed to be doing, I doodle on Henry's homework envelope to cheer him up. His message in capitals looked kind of angry, which is the last thing I want to make him feel right now. I just need him to focus.

When Mom greets me at the school gates—still formally dressed in the red suit jacket and pencil skirt over a frilly black blouse with a black bag and shiny black high heels that she dropped me off in this morning—she actually takes the envelope for Henry out of my hand and carries it all the way to his house for me. I see her studying the picture that I've drawn on the front, frowning a little as I take the envelope back from her at the Xiaos' house.

I ring the doorbell once, before crouching and pushing the envelope under the security door and the front door behind it. The packet of papers is not so fat today, and fits through the gap nicely.

All Mom says as we walk away is "That was quite good, Wen, that picture you did. I used to like to draw too."

I'm still surprised by that as we cross the pedestrian

bridge in silence, heading up the main road and past the local shops. Mom never talks much about herself. I have no idea what she was like when she was little, can't even imagine her or Dad being children. There's just a blank cloudy space where the concept of my parents as children should be. And I've never seen Mom doodle anything in her life. If she ever holds a pen or a pencil, it's usually to write a shopping list with, or to remind herself to pay a bill, in neat standard Chinese characters.

Just before we reach the end of the strip of shops where we have to turn right for home, we hear a single faint scream, followed by Mrs. Xenakis yelling out the doorway of her pharmacy, "Mrs. Zhou! Wen! Help me!" She sounds desperate, not at all like her usual calm self.

Shocked, Mom and I exchange glances, then run inside to find Mrs. Xenakis kneeling on the floor next to an elderly Chinese woman with short, thin grey hair, in a baggy floral blouse and straight brown pants, flat shoes. The old lady is lying on her back on the floor with her eyes closed, and she is clearly struggling to breathe.

"I can't understand what she's saying!" Mrs. Xenakis says anxiously. "Can you just sit with her while I call an ambulance?"

Mom kneels awkwardly in her skirt suit and heels,

placing her black handbag on the floor beside her before hesitantly reaching out and taking the old woman's hand. I do the same on the other side and catch a whiff of fried fish, hairspray and the same musty odor of mold, or damp, that hangs around inside the cupboards of our house.

The bones of the old woman's hands are as light as a bird's, and the loose skin feels papery, as if it's no longer really properly attached to her body. She's whispering something in a Chinese dialect I don't know—it could be a name, or a place, I'm not sure; it's just a jumble of familiar-sounding but incomprehensible noises. But Mom understands, because her face lights up. She starts talking to the old woman in a soothing voice that instantly smooths the sharp crease out of the old woman's forehead. When the ambulance comes to take her away, Mrs. Xenakis directing the paramedics anxiously all the while to be careful, please, she's very frail, the old woman doesn't want to let go of Mom's hand.

"Look, love," says a female paramedic to Mom after trying and failing to break the old woman's grip on Mom's hand, "do you think you could accompany us to the hospital just to get her details down? Help admit her? You'd be doing us a huge favor."

Mom and I exchange anxious looks, suddenly remembering. *No stops!*

This has to be the longest stop on the way home

ever. And if Mom goes to the hospital, what will happen if Dad calls and she's not there?

My voice is anxious as I say, "She can't drive, my mom, she doesn't speak much English herself."

"Someone will run her back, darl," the female ambo says firmly. "I'll make sure of that."

Mom replies, in English, as I stare in surprise, "I speak enough. I can go with you. It's no problem." She digs around with her free hand in her bag and hands me the house keys, which sit cold and heavy in my palm. I've never held them before because no one has ever trusted me to do that.

And I watch, open-mouthed, as Mom—still holding the hand of the old woman, who's now lying on a gurney—is led away from me, saying over her shoulder in Mandarin, "Put the soup on a very low flame and don't add the noodles yet, whatever you do—they'll be too soft. Leave that to me when I get back. And deal with your father. You're clever—you'll know what to say."

Then the paramedics are lifting the gurney into the back of the ambulance and helping Mom and her handbag up into it, and the doors close, and they're all gone.

Mrs. Xenakis and I stand there for a moment in the silent pharmacy, just looking at the empty car spots outside where the ambulance was.

"Well," she says, turning and looking at me, "thank

goodness you and your mom turned up, Wen. I was in a terrible state. I had no idea what to do! You'll be okay to walk home?" She hands me an orange lollipop—the kind she usually gives to little kids who've just had a flu injection—and I nod, still feeling a bit shocked.

Mom's voice was strong, and certain. And she called me *clever*.

In our house *not bad* is the highest praise I think I've ever heard. It's a day for firsts.

Still holding the house keys and the orange lollipop, I turn the corner past the shops into the street that our street runs off, feeling weird that Mom isn't right here with me, my faithful shadow.

There's new graffiti on the side of the pharmacy that proclaims loudly in fluorescent green and pink letters:

And I think, *Yeah, that's what we are. And that's okay.*

CHAPTER 5

ONE STEP, ONE FOOTPRINT

Yībù yīgè jiǎoyìn

THE HOME PHONE IS ALREADY RINGING AS I UN-lock the front door, and my heart sinks. I run towards the kitchen where the phone is, placing the unopened lollipop and the house keys hurriedly down on the kitchen table.

Maybe it's because I don't answer with Mom's tentative *"Wéi?"* that Dad snaps immediately, "Where is your mother? Where is she?" Instantly suspicious that there is something not right in our little world, something is different. Mom knows to answer the telephone every day at four o'clock except on Tuesdays, which is Dad's one day off a week. On Tuesdays he's always home, and the house always feels heavier.

I think quickly, answering in Mandarin, "She's not

feeling well. She's in the bathroom. Food poisoning, something not fresh that she ate."

I'm on high alert, the words just tumbling out. This phone call has the same treacherous feeling as the impromptu debate Miss Spencer sprang on us today—on *why reading is better than TV*—the feeling that things could descend into chaos and shouting at any moment, without warning.

I was on the side of TV, and our side *crushed* the reading side because TV has more people like Nikki Kuol and me and even horrible Billy Raum in it. We pointed out that there are Aboriginal people on TV (whose land this was, is and always will be—I mean, how stupid do you have to be to think being here a few decades, or even a couple of centuries, gives you more right to this place than the people who've been here for thousands of years?), while there aren't many Aboriginal people in books, at least not the books we have in the school library. My team said all that, to general cheering.

Everyone agreed that books without real people in them were *dumb* (their word, not mine—I would have said, possibly, *boring* or *rather far-fetched*) and even Miss Spencer was laughing by the end, although she pretended to be outraged that TV had won hands down over reading.

"Philistines!" she laughed.

"But *are* we?" Gabriella Amato called out. "Are we really, if the medium itself is refusing to move with the times?" And we all laughed harder, feeling clever and a bit wicked.

Miss Spencer had replied with a huge smile, "I actually have great hope for this world yet, thanks to you people."

"Your mother is so unwell that she can't come to the phone?" Dad asks now, incredulously, and I say in English, as cheerfully as I can manage, "Better out than in, Dad. That's what the school nurse always says."

In his usual way, Dad doesn't say goodbye, he just makes a snorting noise, then hangs up.

He calls again half an hour later, when Mom is still not home, and this time he threatens to drive home to check on her, even though his shift at Hai Tong Tai has only just started and he'll get in all sorts of trouble if he leaves. I tell him she's sleeping now, and that I'll get her to call as soon as she wakes up.

"What about your dinner?" he barks, and I reply quietly, "She made it earlier today, like she always does, because she's prepared, and a good mother."

I pause, thinking about Fay Xiao and all the things people said about her before she died, and are still saying about her now that she's dead. I take a deep breath.

"We'll eat together as soon as Mom . . ." I almost say *gets back* but say instead "gets out of bed."

I hear shouting in Cantonese in the distance, and Dad abruptly slams down the phone.

When he calls yet again, another precise half-hour later, I'm feeling desperate. There's no more *clever* left in the tank.

"Wake her for me!" Dad's voice is brusque. "I need to talk to her. If it's serious, I need to take her to hospital. To see a *doctor.*" The emphasis on that last word is bitter, as if he'd actually said *real doctor* instead of just *doctor*.

Having burned off the medical side of himself, Dad never tries to treat any of us anymore. *I have no opinions on health matters in any shape or form*, he says brusquely, when I try to ask him about a cut, or a sore throat. *I'm not "appropriately qualified."* When Dad failed the specialist pathway exams the fourth time, I think he threw away all his textbooks and medical equipment in a fit of boiling fury, or maybe he built a bonfire with them and watched them burn to ashes too. But deep down, he's still a man of science, and I can tell he's worried. It's so out of character for Mom to be sick, or asleep any time before he gets home instead of waiting anxiously for him to return, that I know my cover story is about to fall apart.

"I . . . uh," I reply.

"Wake her up," Dad insists. "I want to talk to her *now*, Wen."

I put the receiver down on the table and actually walk to the front of the house and pull the curtains aside and look through the windows. I even slam a few doors and open a few drawers loudly near the receiver before I pick it up again.

"She's in the bathroom again," I say bravely. "She'll call you back as soon as she's out."

"She can't do that, you silly girl,"—Dad's voice is the iciest I've ever heard it—"because I'm in the middle of the busiest shift we've had this week. Get her *now*."

I almost jump out of my skin—I actually drop the receiver on the kitchen bench with a *bang*—when Mom walks through the kitchen door with a questioning look as I'm standing there, panicking. I point hurriedly at my tummy, and my forehead, as she runs forward, seeing my stricken expression. She sets her shiny black handbag down on a benchtop and picks up the phone.

A whole range of emotions flashes across her face as Dad shouts at her down the phone like he's not a person but a machine gun with words for bullets. I'm still standing there pointing at my tummy and making eating-with-a-spoon gestures in front of my face, pretending to retch, as Mom replies calmly, "Yes, yes, much better," and "No, no, I don't need to see a doctor—it seems to have passed. The nap?" She looks at me questioningly. "It did me a lot of good. I feel almost myself again."

After she puts down the phone we stare at each other for a long moment, caught out in a shared act of subterfuge, or self-protection, maybe our first ever. Then Mom seems to give herself a mental shake, moves her handbag to a kitchen chair, takes off her red jacket— looking more crumpled and stained than it ever has before—and straps on her black apron.

"Get the packet of lā miàn from the refrigerator," she says as she turns up the burner flame on the soup she's been brewing all day, taking out a separate pot to boil the noodles in.

Mom is very quiet as we walk towards Henry's house after dinner. When we get there, it's a lot later than the time we stopped at the Xiaos' house yesterday. Mom says fretfully, "I hope they haven't already eaten. Ring the bell, Wen."

I ring the bell and nothing happens for a while, so I ring it again. Standing there, on the dark front porch, Mom and I wonder if anyone will even come to the door today.

I know the set of three steel food carriers Mom is holding is heavy. She hasn't just made dinner for Henry, she's made enough for his father, too.

In the bottom tier of the carrier is the rich broth Mom has made from the gǒu qǐ or goji berries, lotus root, carrots, mushrooms, dried longan, dried scallops and fresh chicken. She even added a handful of dried white fungus for nourishment and for clearing the lungs, she said. In the second tier is the boneless chicken meat she shredded for them, together with the other ingredients. And in the top tier are the glistening white noodles, or lā miàn, that Mom boiled for less than two minutes, so that they won't be too soft to eat when the hot broth is added to them.

I'm about to press the doorbell one more time when the light over the front step snaps on. The wooden front door behind the security door opens and a faint bit of light streams out around the slightly bent figure of a man watching us from behind the wire mesh.

"Zhou Tài tài," the man says heavily. Mrs. Zhou.

Dad once explained to me that Tài tài is an honorific

that means "rich lady who does not work" because no one would consider housework and raising children actual work. *It's just what women do*, Dad had added, snapping his newspaper open.

I remember, quite distinctly, thinking, *Well, no one's ever going to call me Tài tài, if that's what it means.*

"Wen," Henry's dad adds politely but warily, still not opening the screen door, just studying us through it.

Mom addresses him in formal Mandarin. "Mr. Xiao," she says in a rush. "Apologies for our rude intrusion, but would you take the trouble to eat the dinner we have prepared for you? It is not what you are used to, it is very plain and ordinary, but we would be grateful if you would at least try some. And Henry. Wen says it is important that he keeps his strength up. For study." She lifts her burden of cooked food a little higher so that Henry's dad is forced to look at it through the wire door.

"I'm not sure if *study* is what is harming Henry, or keeping him from harm," Mr. Xiao rasps in reply. "He will not eat. He will not sleep. He will not leave his bedroom. The only food he has taken for the last two days was the piece of fish you kindly left him yesterday." "There's an entrance exam," I remind the dark silhouette through the wire, afraid that Henry's dad will shut the door before I can make him understand how important it is. "It's just over a week from now. If Henry wins that place, Mr. Xiao, anything is possible. The best education, but for hardly any money. Our teacher, Miss Spencer, says that Henry can get in, that that school will give him wings. Did you know that he wants to build airplanes one day . . . ?"

"Ahhh," Mr. Xiao murmurs when I falter to a stop. "I had forgotten the exam. Henry and I never talk much, you know. He is like me, not very talkative, and now . . ." I hear the deep sadness in his voice.

Beside me, Mom hefts the steel food carriers a little higher, her thin arms straining with the weight of the rapidly cooling food.

Mr. Xiao finally unlocks the screen door and opens it a fraction, not wide enough that we can see all of him, although what we can see of his face and person is pretty bad. He looks very pale, unshaven, his short salt-and-pepper hair uncombed and standing on end, wearing a stained T-shirt and trousers as if he's come straight from the market, although it's almost bedtime.

"Hot broth," Mom explains quickly as she urges Henry's dad to take the steel food carriers from her. "A bit of meat, vegetable, noodles, all healthy things. Put all the food in a bowl for you, a bowl for Henry, and pour the broth over the top. But it must be very hot," she adds. "And tell Henry to drink all of it—the soup is very good for you, very nourishing. I made it especially for him, because he is growing."

Mr. Xiao takes the carriers from Mom, and I see her shoulders droop slightly in relief. She hadn't expected him to take them. Everyone knows that the Xiaos are very poor, but also that they are very proud; though not in a bad or boastful way. They've just never asked anyone for help, even though Fay Xiao was clearly struggling, Mr. Xiao can't afford to buy a car and drives his second cousin's vegetable delivery truck everywhere, and Henry's always looked like a gust of wind will blow him away.

"Thank you, Mrs. Zhou," Mr. Xiao says quietly. "We will not forget your kindness, Henry and I." His grip on the food carriers is awkward as he holds the screen door open with just his foot. "Henry did mention before my wife, before Mrs. Xiao . . ." He doesn't finish the sentence, but starts another one. "Henry did mention that you're sitting the entrance exam together, Wen. I'd be honored to take you both to the school on the day of the exam. It will save your parents the long drive."

I go instantly hot, not daring to look at my mother beside me.

Mr. Xiao turns away and locks the security door

once more, murmuring through the wire, "Thank you, thank you," before shutting the wooden door. The light over the front porch snaps off.

Mom turns to me slowly in the dark, wide-eyed. "What entrance exam?"

PART TWO

Meng Yi Tzu asked about being filial. The
Master answered, "Never fail to comply."

— Confucius, *The Analects*, Book II, 5

Tzu-chang asked about the way of the good
man. The Master said, "Such a man does
not follow in other people's footsteps."

— Confucius, *The Analects*, Book XI, 20

CHAPTER 6

THE RIGHT PATH

WHEN MOM AND I REACH HENRY'S HOUSE ON Saturday after my morning sessions of Chinese school and extra maths tuition, the set of steel food containers is there on the porch, washed and dried and smelling of lemons. But the envelope of homework from Miss Spencer isn't, and when I look around for it, even poking around in the bushes out the front of Henry's house in case it's blown away, Mom murmurs, "Even Henry deserves a rest on Saturday, Wen. Leave it now."

"He'd better not be giving up," I mutter in reply as we walk away with the set of food carriers. Mom doesn't reply. After I told her about the entrance exam on our walk home from the Xiaos' house last night, about how Miss Spencer thought we might even have a chance, she was very quiet. As we reached our driveway, all she said was "He will never let you go." But she hadn't said *No* to the idea completely, and that gave me hope.

When we pass the open door of Mrs. Xenakis's pharmacy, she waves at us while she's serving a customer. I see that she notices the set of steel food containers in Mom's hands, because her eyes narrow briefly in thought before she laughs at something the woman says, and turns away to ring up the purchase.

After we've arrived home and eaten a quick lunch of egg noodles fried with strips of pork, fresh garlic chives and dried black mushrooms, Mom sets about making dinner for us, but also for Henry and his dad. She prepares a hearty stew out of chunks of beef brisket, carrots, turnips, onion and potatoes that she simmers all afternoon until the gravy is thick and shiny; flavored with things like mushroom soy, shào xīng wine, garlic cloves, ginger and star anise. Before we sit down to eat our own dinner, we walk back to Henry's house and leave a big saucepan of stew for them, together with more rice than two people can possibly eat. No one comes to the door when we ring the bell, and there's still no envelope of finished homework on the front step. The Xiaos' house looks even smaller and meaner in the late afternoon sunshine as Mom and I walk away from it, empty-handed.

On Sunday, when Mom and I drop by in the afternoon with a large earthenware pot filled to the brim with pork belly braised with finger eggplant and seasoned with garlic, chili, spring onions and chunks of dried salted fish, together with another huge serving of rice, we are met with the two saucepans we left the day before, carefully washed and dried. The envelope of homework from Miss Spencer is there this time, sitting under the saucepans. Like the envelope before it, all the worksheets inside are carefully completed.

After I've slid all the papers back inside with a feeling of relief that Henry is still on track, still focused on *the dream*, Mom turns the envelope over gently in my hands and says quietly, "Henry has left you some homework of your own. Make sure you do it properly, Wen."

In red pencil, on the back of the envelope, he's written out four long division maths equations. My heart sinks. I know I'm supposed to have them done by the end of Monday, to slip back under the front door after school for Henry to correct. It will take me most of lunchtime tomorrow to get through them, because long division is the worst. To do long division you have to know all your times tables, and I'm not sure that I do. I like to think that I'm affected by selective times tables amnesia. Even with all the extra worksheets Miss Spencer has been giving me, and Saturday tuition, maths is like wading through quicksand. If I flap around too much, I feel like I'm drowning. If I attempt it slowly, I still feel like I'm drowning.

As we turn the corner to go home holding Henry's homework and the clean saucepans, Mrs. Xenakis shoots out of the pharmacy in her white lab coat, standing right between us and the corner so that we have to stop walking. I'm conscious that Mom and I are each holding a piece of cookware, in the street, in broad daylight, because an elderly woman with a shopping trolley turns to stare at the three of us as she passes. Mrs. Xenakis tries very hard not to stare at the saucepans and is very friendly, but determined. She asks if Mom can stop by the pharmacy on the way home from school on Monday afternoon.

Mom's expression is immediately wary.

"Say, three-forty-five?" Mrs. Xenakis adds quickly. "It won't take long. Just a small, quick favor."

Mom, surprised, nods slowly. She likes Mrs. Xenakis, who is one of the few English-speaking shopkeepers in the local shopping strip that Mom doesn't feel uncomfortable talking to. A lot of the others treat Mom as if she's slow or hard of hearing, even though Mom is as quick as a bird.

That afternoon, when Dad rings home to check on us, I notice that Mom doesn't mention the small, quick favor at all, although I hear her deny that there is anything wrong, that she's just tired, more than once.

When I reach my locker on Monday morning, Nikki, rocking a denim onesie under her school sweatshirt, with her beautiful braids pulled into a low side pony, and Fatima, who's wearing a pretty dark-red headscarf today with a sparkly border over her usual school sweat-shirt and jeans, are standing there smiling. Nikki is holding a navy sports bag in a thin shiny fabric, the kind you buy from a two-dollar shop that can fold back up into a tiny purse. "Miss Spencer mentioned that you and your mom are bringing Henry food and homework, which is *amazing*," Nikki says.

"Not the homework," Fatima laughs, elbowing her. "The homework's not amazing."

Nikki shoots her a look that says, *Can we be serious for a moment here, please?* "My mom," she continues, holding the bag out to me, "heard about Henry and wanted to help." She shakes the end of her ponytail of fine braids off her shoulder and looks at me squarely.

"We *all* want to help," Fatima says, not laughing any-more. "But as you guys have the food part covered—"

"And we weren't sure if Henry likes South Sudanese food," Nikki interjects.

"Or North Sudanese food," Fatima adds, "or has even tried it, our moms, and some of the other moms, thought that Henry might need, like, *things*, you know?" Fatima's voice is somber. "Like clothes. It's getting cold. So we did a small collection."

My eyes drop to the navy sports bag as Nikki unzips it and Fatima rifles around inside, showing me what's in there, the five thin gold bracelets on her wrist jingling.

"Some trousers," she says, and we all glance at each other, thinking of Henry's painfully exposed ankles.

"Two warm jumpers," Fatima continues, "because it's really starting to get cold."

"Some T-shirts," Nikki adds. "Because maybe his dad isn't doing much laundry at the moment?"

"Loads of socks, but no shoes," Fatima says apologetically, "because we weren't sure what size Henry's feet are. But we can get some, if you can find out? My uncle has a shoe shop." She zips the bag back up. "It's no trouble. We've already worded him up and he said Henry can have his pick of the store, any color, any style, he just has to go in and choose."

They help me jam my backpack and the shiny sports bag into my locker and we walk into the classroom together, all smiling, but also feeling a bit like we want to cry. None of us can imagine how it would feel to be Henry right now. Not with our moms at home, doing mom stuff, the way they always do, day in, day out.

Miss Spencer sees us come in together and smiles, holding her hand out for Henry's work. I slide all the worksheets out carefully and return them to her, saying, "I'll give you back the envelope at the end of the day, if that's okay? Henry's left me some maths exercises." I turn the envelope over and show her the four maths problems in red pencil.

"Answer them carefully, Wen," she laughs. "But in a way that will keep Henry 'talking'!"

And we grin at each other in understanding, before I take my seat between Nikki and Fatima, who've saved me a spot.

At lunchtime, everyone is out on the dusty oval or hanging around near the climbing frames and outdoor gym equipment under the bedraggled eucalyptus trees— everyone except me. I'm in the library, surrounded by this week's usual book display of girls with long flowing golden hair in colorful ballgowns, or the headless torsos of girls with long flowing golden hair in colorful ballgowns, trying to work my way through the long division questions as quickly as possible so that I can go out and sit in the thin sunshine with my friends.

How do I answer Henry's questions in a way that will keep Henry "talking?" To me *and* to Miss Spencer?

I think about all the ways that long division doesn't make sense to me—how I can never tell which bit is the divisor or the dividend or the quotient, or what numbers to bring down, and where to put them exactly.

But I don't want to completely *enrage* Henry—I just need to keep him engaged, even if it's just in numbers. So I do my best to solve the four equations he's set me, leaving just the one obvious thing wrong with each answer, groaning as the bell goes for period five. As expected, the whole exercise has taken forever, and I've had no lunch, no sun and no chats. Stomach rumbling, I search out Miss Spencer and hand her the empty envelope with the desperate scribble all over it.

She calls out as I'm hurrying away, "But, Wen, you forgot the—"

And I raise my hand, shouting, "I *know!*" and her face breaks into a wide grin, as she works out what I've done, on purpose. Miss Spencer waves the wrinkled envelope back at me in farewell as I hurry to French class.

That afternoon, after Mom and I have dropped the bag full of clothes for Henry with a note tucked inside that says it's from the Kuol, Salah, Deng and Abango families, together with the fresh batch of homework, we stop at Mrs. Xenakis's pharmacy at precisely 3:45 p.m.

The old Chinese woman Mom helped the other day is standing inside by the counter, next to an equally old wrinkly-faced man with hollow cheeks dressed in a faded brown three-piece suit with widely spaced, thin stripes. Both elderly people are smiling, and the woman reaches out and catches one of Mom's hands in hers and begins shaking it warmly.

Mom's face breaks up into smiley lines as she chats to them in Shanghainese while Mrs. Xenakis and I look on, grinning. Mom explained, when she got home from the hospital the other afternoon, that the old woman lived with her daughter's family and was from Shanghai, and didn't speak any other languages.

"My third uncle's wife was from Shanghai," Mom told me with a faraway look. "I really loved that aunty, but she died just before I went to high school. We used to spend hours in the kitchen together when I was small because she cooked for the whole family. All of us lived in the one house, all the uncles and aunties and cousins, and because she was the best cook, she did all the cooking, for everyone."

"Didn't she mind?" I asked, my feelings about cooking being lukewarm at best.

Mom replied, "Everyone was expected to do what they were expected to do."

"No arguments," I added flatly.

"These are different times," Mom replied quietly. "Strange times. That time and this time are like two different countries separated by an insurmountable wall. Not everything from one makes sense in the other. I really miss that aunty. And her cooking."

Mom turns to Mrs. Xenakis now and says, "Mr. and Mrs. Wu agree that they must take better care of their health. What do you suggest they do, Mrs. Xenakis? They trust your opinion very much."

"Well, now that winter is approaching," Mrs. Xenakis replies immediately, "they should consider getting a flu shot each. I've had no way to ask them if they've had them done already. I can arrange that for them tomorrow, if they'd like—can you tell them that?"

Mom translates Mrs. Xenakis's words and the old couple smiles and nods. When they say something to Mom in their language, I see something in Mom's face change and she shakes her head quickly, replying in Shanghainese in a way that makes Mrs. Wu's face fall, and Mr. Wu look worried.

Mrs. Xenakis says, "What is it, Mrs. Zhou? What's the problem? Tell them it won't cost them anything, if that's what they're worried about."

Mom shakes her head, replying hastily, "It's not the cost, Mrs. Xenakis. It's just that Mrs. Wu wants me to be here tomorrow, so that I can translate when you give her and her husband the injection. But I can't. It's Tuesday."

Mrs. Xenakis looks confused. Mom glances at me, her eyes asking me to explain.

I say quickly, "It's Dad's one day off, every week. We always eat dinner together and there's a lot of . . ." Mom and I exchange looks again. ". . . preparation, a lot of work, involved. Mom and me are supposed to get back from school by four o'clock every day. No stops. But *especially* on Tuesdays."

It sounds ridiculous when I say it out loud.

Mom glances at her watch now, as do I. It's 3:54 p.m. We need to get home, for the call.

Mrs. Xenakis frowns, and her reply is swift. "Tell Mrs. Wu we'll do the flu shot on Wednesday, at three-forty-five, then." She looks from me to Mom, adding, "Is that all right? You'd be doing me another great favor, Mrs. Zhou. I have a lot of elderly Chinese customers, and it's a real struggle to get across everything that I want to say . . ."

The uncertain look is back on Mom's face—the look she wears when she's faced with a Chinese restaurant menu with too many pages and Dad is waiting, impatiently, for a decision. At this point, Mom usually lets someone else decide for her.

So I do.

"That's fine," I cut in, before Mom can object, and she gives me a sharp, sideways glance but doesn't disagree. "I'll make sure she's here at three-forty-five on Wednesday, Mrs. X."

Mom translates for the Wus, and they nod, their faces relaxing, happy again.

"See you on Wednesday," Mrs. Xenakis says to the old couple, and to Mom, bowing low from the waist, and I giggle.

"We only do that on special occasions now, Mrs. Xenakis. The bowing."

"This *is* a special occasion," Mrs. Xenakis replies thoughtfully as she straightens. "There's a lot I could learn from you and your mom, Wen."

Mom gently withdraws her hand from Mrs. Wu's, and we back out of the shop, still waving.

CHAPTER 7

EIGHT DISHES FOR LUCK

ON TUESDAY MORNING, WHEN WE STOP BY HENRY'S house on the way to school, the clean pot from the dinner we dropped over on Monday night is there on the front porch, plus the usual finished envelope of homework. Mom's face suddenly changes when we reach the school gates. "The pot!" we both say at the same time, looking down at the clean metal saucepan in Mom's hands. It's one of her medium-sized ones, but it's still big.

"If I come back from school holding an empty pot, he will see, and ask questions," Mom exclaims, troubled.

"It's too hard to explain," I agree, "what you're doing, going for a morning walk with a huge pot. Let me put it in my schoolbag."

"It will be too heavy," Mom replies fretfully in Chinese, wringing her hands.

"No it won't," I reply firmly, already shoving the pot in under my PE clothes. "It won't be any trouble at all."

It *is* heavy, when I shove the bag into my locker in the morning. And it's awkward trying to fit stuff in around the pot all day without crumpling things too badly, but I'll do anything to keep that look off Mom's face. I swear to myself that I will never allow that expression to cross my own features.

When we drop an envelope of fresh homework at Henry's house, ringing the bell once and sliding the envelope under the door like we always do, Mom hurries us away quickly. "I have a lot to do," she says, and her voice is distracted, the way it always is on Tuesdays.

After we get home, I slide the pot out of my bag and into its usual place in the kitchen. Then I practice halfheartedly, but quietly, on the secondhand electronic keyboard in my bedroom and vaguely wave my violin bow at my horrible, scratchy, school-issue violin for the minimum amount of time I can get away with before sitting down at the kitchen table to do my homework. The whole time Dad relaxes in the sitting room, in front of the TV, which is on very loud.

Mom turns the heat up slightly under the rich broth she's been simmering all day out of pork ribs, fish bones, dried scallops, dried figs, dried black mushrooms, slices of ginger and a curl of dried tangerine peel. I watch as she drops handfuls of dried beancurd skins into the soup before busily preparing a fillet of white fish for steaming in a bamboo basket with soy, shào xīng wine and a handful of garlic, ginger, coriander and spring onions seasoned with black pepper and sesame oil. There's a mound of sliced beef for frying with onions, a plate of green vegetables to be tossed in a searing wok with oyster sauce and garlic, and there's rice, perfectly measured for three hungry people, already cooking in a separate claypot. A piece of pork belly is roasting in the oven, the crackling already nice and bubbly, the fat rendered out. At the back of the stove, a claypot containing chunks of sticky, marinated pumpkin with dried shrimp is being kept warm, while beside it another claypot full of pork mince, spring onion and chunks of tofu in a light gravy is simmering on a very low flame.

While I frown and mutter through two pages of probability, percentages and decimals, Mom is a blur of chopping, stirring, ladling and straining, her spatula repeatedly striking the surface of the smoking wok like the hooves of a mythical beast striking an iron roadway.

She finally turns off the exhaust fan over the stove.

"Call your father to eat," she says anxiously, taking her black apron off and hanging it on its customary hook by the kitchen door. I rise, shoving my homework into a dark corner of the kitchen bench, beside the fridge, so that no one will ask to see it and helpfully point out every single one of my errors.

The doorbell rings before I even reach the TV room. Skin prickling with alarm—visitors that aren't Jehovah's Witnesses or LED lightbulb salespeople being rare at our place—I watch from the hall as Dad answers the door.

It's Nikki Kuol, standing outside our wire security screen, and my face breaks into a smile. She's holding a colorful piece of paper in one hand and looking around—at our small front yard where Mom grows Chinese vegetables in neat rows in one bed, at the palm-sized red, green and gold octagonal mirror that Mom placed on our security door when we first moved in, which is now worn and peeling from years of exposure to the elements.

I reach the door behind Dad as Nikki says through the wire, "Hello? Wen?"

She's still wearing our school sweatshirt over the same denim skirt and runners without socks that she had on today at school, but she's let her amazing hair down. All the long, glossy black braids are falling across

94

her shoulders and spilling down her back. Nikki's voice sounds puffed, as if she's run all the way from her house.

"Yes?" Dad says icily, not opening the security door.

Surprising myself, I reach around Dad and unsnib the lock, opening the door wide enough so that Nikki can see us, and we can see her, properly.

None of my friends has ever come to my house before.

Nikki blinks at the sight of the two us standing there and smiles. "Hi, Wen," she says quickly. "Mr. Zhou."

Dad doesn't reply, but a huge grin breaks across my face as Nikki hands me the piece of bright paper in her hand. It's an invitation. I've heard some other girls talking about Nikki's party for the last couple of weeks, always stifling a spurt of jealousy that Nikki didn't bother to ask me, even though we hang together all the time.

Nikki's words tumble out, as if she too can feel the wave of coldness coming from my father. "It's my birthday party on Sunday. Just at the scout hall?" Nikki points down the road. "From one in the afternoon. There'll be a live band, Wen, and my cousin, Bol, he's just come back from a world skateboarding championship in Japan and is showing us his new promo video! He's got a new sponsorship deal. His Korean girlfriend, who's a skater too, is coming. It would be amazing if you could, uh, join us. You too, Mr. Zhou—Mom and Dad would love to meet you and Mrs. Zhou, and there'll be plenty of food. It will just end when it ends. You could leave whenever . . ."

Nikki's voice trails off as Dad pulls the invitation out of my fingers, scanning it quickly. He folds it over and doesn't give it back to me. "Thank you, Nikki," he says pleasantly, "but Wen will be helping her mother at home that day. She will be too busy to come."

Then he gives Nikki this tight little nod, pulls the screen door out of my hand and shuts it in Nikki's face. Her shocked expression is probably the exact same one I'm wearing.

"Thanks, Nikki, see you tom—" I just manage to get out before Dad shuts the wooden door and cuts me off completely.

I spin around, so angry that I feel as if I'm going to burst into flames.

Dad seems to fill the hallway. It's him staring down at me staring up at him and I'm so rage-filled, and sad, that I almost hear something inside me . . . separate. Like my mind has gone outside my body completely, and is looking at it wondering what it's going to do next.

Dad has this half smile on his face—the same half smile he always wears just before he loses his temper, or lashes out with whatever he's holding, or slams his hand into the surface of a table or a door or a wall, and I know what he's going to say before he even says it. The words seem to come at me in slow motion, or as if I've already heard them, and I'm just standing inside a memory; because I've been hearing them all my life.

"This is for your own good, Zhou Wen Li," says Dad, in the same bland and pleasant tone he used on Nikki. "No parties. This is for your own protection. It is your job to obey, my job to keep you safe."

From what? The dangerous dangers of a birthday party? I want to shout.

I actually have to bite down, hard, on my tongue so that no words come out.

"Wen?" Mom calls anxiously from the kitchen doorway at the end of the hall. "Jin? Dinner's getting cold. What are you two doing?"

Not forgetting! I almost scream, my fists clenched so tight that my nails are cutting deep half-moons into my palms. *I am in the process of not forgetting any of this, Mom, for the rest of my life!*

I turn on my heel, entering the kitchen before Dad does, in silence. I want to punch a wall too, slam my fist into the surface of the kitchen table. But I don't, because it doesn't help anything, and who knows what would happen if I did?

You are not him, I tell myself over and over so that I do not cry, *and you will never be like him. Make sure of that.*

As Dad seats himself at the kitchen table, carefully dressed in the buttoned-up business shirt and pressed trousers he insists on wearing even though it's his day off, Mom places all the dishes she's been trying to keep warm on the table with exaggerated care. One Tuesday night, she dropped a full tray of roasted chicken at Dad's feet, by accident, the pieces going all over the floor, which he then refused to touch, pointedly eating just rice and vegetables; even though she rinsed and reheated the chicken, almost in tears. Mom has never done that again.

She slides a bowl of mounded steamed rice in front of each of us now, inviting us to eat, picking up a serving spoon while she waits for Dad to pick up his chopsticks. She always serves Dad and me first, before she turns to her own meal.

Dad's eyes narrow as he surveys the table. "There are only *seven* dishes," he says flatly.

I watch the color rise in Mom's cheeks as her eyes fly around the serving bowls and plates in the centre of the table—soup, beef, fish, roast pork, vegetables, pumpkin, tofu. You don't ever count the rice as a dish; it's just an accompaniment, not a main. Mom has miscounted. Seven is an unlucky number of dishes. Even I know that.

Quickly rising, her cheeks flooded hot with color, Mom grabs a small serving plate from the cupboard beside the stove and places some of the slices of roasted pork onto it so that there are now eight dishes on the table in front of us. Her hands are unsteady as she picks up her serving spoon again, repeating her careful invitation to us all to eat.

Giving her a hard look, Dad indicates with a nod that he wants a serving of fish first. He begins eating steadily, telling Mom that the soup isn't salty enough, but the pumpkin is too salty. "The beef is tough," he notes, "and very roughly sliced, and the vegetables are overcooked, as is the roast pork. And this fish!" he exclaims. "Couldn't you buy a whole fresh fish? There's barely enough for one person, let alone three."

Mom seems to have grown smaller in her chair. "We never finish a whole fish," she murmurs. "I didn't want to waste any food, like we always do."

"You've run out of housekeeping money again, haven't you?" Dad asks. "*Haven't you?* What are you spending my money on?"

He gets up and opens the fridge door and we can all see straight through to the back. There are a few pieces of fruit in a bowl, half a loaf of sliced bread and some slices of ham for my school lunches, a few spring onions, a piece of meat defrosting on a plate under clingwrap, a container of milk, a packet of dried scallops and a half-empty bag of dried black beans. He looks in the freezer. "What have you done with all the money I gave you for this month? There's barely any food in the house!"

Mom is about to answer, looking like she's about to blurt out everything we've been doing for Henry and his dad, when I interrupt cheerfully, "I've eaten it!" My voice sounds unnaturally loud in our fake-wood-panelled kitchen. "All the food! Growth spurt. You should see me after school, Dad. *Whoo.*"

Dad looks me up and down, suspiciously, before closing the freezer door and sitting down again. He picks up his rice bowl in his left hand, chopsticks in his right. "You don't seem any different to me," he says sharply. "And neither do your maths results. Finish eating, Wen, and help your mother to clean up."

When Dad's done, he just pushes away from the table, walks out of the room and sits back down in front of the TV like he always does. I hear it go on, a studio audience somewhere far away screaming with laughter.

As I carry our rice bowls to the sink, Mom pulls washing gloves on with hands that are shaking slightly.

"Every day is like a test," she mutters as she begins filling the sink with washing water, "a difficult test it is impossible to study for. Especially Tuesdays. What are the questions?" Her laughter sounds strained as she scrubs at the rice bowls, piling them up on the draining board for me to wipe. "What are the answers? Who knows?"

She leans forward for a moment, gripping the edge of the sink with both her gloved hands, and murmurs in Mandarin, *"Only with death does the road come to an end. Is that not long?"*

"Mom!" I reply in English, sharp with fear, thinking of Henry's mom, how she must have taken those words, written more than two thousand years ago, completely literally. "Honestly! Now you're beginning to sound like Dad with all the unrelenting negativity. *Stop it.*"

But my hands are shaking too as I dry all the things she's washed. Handwashing dishes takes forever on Tuesdays, even though it's just the three of us. The effort never seems proportionate to the meal—it feels like three bites and it's all gone and what was all that really for? Before the endless washing begins.

Mom continues to stand there, staring down into the washing water, her eyes very bright, the bubbles breaking and re-forming.

I want to ask her if there is a different way to be.

Where you can take all the good things about what you are, what's expected of you, and leave behind all the stuff that holds you back. But I'm afraid of the answer; I'm afraid of being so disappointed that it will feel like my heart is being ripped out, so I don't ask.

Mom returns to washing the dishes, not speaking.

Remembering, I put down my dishcloth for a moment, scooping the leftover rice on the sideboard into a plastic container with what's left of the tofu and minced pork, slices of roast pork and sticky braised pumpkin. "It's not much," I say, working quickly to pile the leftovers in beside the rice so that Mom can wash all the serving plates, "but at least it's something."

Mom's eyes widen and her gloved hands fall still in the sudsy water when she works out what I'm doing. "You can't take that to Henry, Wen. We can't go out. Not today. It's too hard."

I think of Dad shutting the door in Nikki's startled face, in mine, cutting us off from each other and all the words we were in the middle of saying, and my mouth tightens.

"But Henry will think that we've forgotten him!" I exclaim. "Him and his dad. Maybe he hasn't eaten all day. Maybe they don't have any food in the house, have you thought of that?"

"We've given them what food we had in *our* house,"

Mom reminds me under her breath. "Even your father has noticed that. Henry will have to manage for one day. I'm sorry, but your father puts our family first before all others. The Xiao family is not our family, that's what your father will say if he sees you doing this. He won't like it. I don't want any more trouble, Wen, *please*. Not for me, not for you."

I feel anger flare up in me again, sharp and hot and choking. Mom's right—life's a test, and the rules are unknowable, the reasons for them just the same, and I'll be in trouble no matter what, no matter when, *so—*

Test me.

If I can't go to a party, I can at least help a friend in trouble who lives only, what, three or four hundred meters away.

I snap the lid onto the plastic container with unnecessary force and slide the box into a plastic bag. "I'm going," I say before Mom can protest. "I'll be back before Dad even knows I'm gone. The TV's so loud he won't even hear the front door opening and closing. Make lots of noise putting the dishes away. Pretend you're talking to me, I don't know."

"Wen?" Mom hisses fearfully, but I'm already sliding into a pair of outdoor shoes and heading for the front door with the plastic bag containing its box of leftover dinner.

Maybe I make too much noise, or maybe there's a fiendish tracking device implanted just beneath the surface of my skin that gives out signals as to my whereabouts, but Dad is already turning and rising out of his armchair as I go past the lounge room door.

"Wen!" he snaps. "Where are you going?"

"For a walk!" I call from the hall, more bravely than I'm feeling, my hand already releasing the security door chain on the front door. As Dad comes out of the lounge room, I quickly slide the plastic bag I'm holding onto a hook on our hallstand, covering it hastily with an overcoat.

I give him an enquiring look, saying too fast, "I ate too much. I'll be exactly five minutes. Just up to the end of the shops and back. Exercise is good for you. You don't want me to get fat."

Dad looks at me suspiciously. "It's cold outside. And dark. It's dangerous. I'll come with you."

I get the shivers, imagining me and Dad actually walking to Henry's house, crossing that big concrete bridge over all the traffic, and me having to explain why, and us having to talk to each other about all the things I'm failing to do properly, and not talking about all the things Dad could be doing with his life instead of serving ungrateful people tea with bad grace at the Hai Tong Tai Seafood Restaurant. We don't talk much, ever, because Dad doesn't listen. He just tells me what to do and how to do it. No arguments.

Sure, every day might be a test, but every moment we spend together is a lecture.

I want to scream, *Dad, our lives are completely joyless! Don't you get that? Don't you want to change it?*

Before I actually open my mouth to do it, Mom hurries into the hall without her washing gloves on, her hands still red from the scalding washing water. "I'll take her," she says quickly, reaching for a jacket. "You've been working all week, Jin, and you're tired."

"It's dangerous," Dad says, frowning, "to leave home—especially for people like you, and especially at night. What's gotten into you?"

Mom and I look at each other, look down.

"You're not going out," Dad says with finality, sensing some hidden purpose, but not knowing what it is. He looks at each of us with narrowed eyes, at our empty hands and shadowed expressions. "You should know better."

But what he's really saying is *I know better.*

"Your mother's right, Wen," he adds, his voice harsh. "I'm tired, and a walk in the cold is the last thing I want to do on the one night off that I am permitted each week! Now finish your work, *both of you.*" Then he walks across to the front door and chains it firmly before sitting himself back down in front of the television.

Mom must have retrieved the plastic bag of food from the hallway stand, because when I wake up in the morning and put my jacket on to go to school, the bag is gone and the plastic container is empty, clean and dry. Back in its usual place in the bottom drawer; below the cutlery drawer, and the one for tea towels.

CHAPTER 8

SOMETHING FROM NOTHING

WHEN WE PICK UP THE ENVELOPE OF FINISHED homework on Wednesday morning, I can't help smiling.

Henry has simply circled each of the remainders that I deliberately forgot to include in my answers to the four long division questions, in the same red pencil that he wrote the questions in.

Amazingly, I didn't get anything else wrong. So maybe it's starting to make sense. And Henry doesn't know this, but the remainders I actually got wrong on purpose.

When I turn the envelope over, my heart sinks to my shoes. Written on the back of the envelope is the longest long division question I've ever seen. Even Mom raises her eyebrows at how long it is. Now Henry is just being cruel. It's going to take at least half of recess to get through this one.

There's nothing else from Henry, though. No angry note about us maybe forgetting to leave him any dinner last night. No anatomically precise and detailed doodles of dragons or warriors that are always perfectly proportioned, which put my messy people and animals to shame.

But at least Henry is still up to communicating in numbers and symbols, and that's okay by me. I need to keep his thoughts away from that twisted apple tree in his backyard, whatever I do.

On an impulse, I slide out all of Henry's finished homework, handing it to Mom to hold. Then I scribble my answer to the long division question on the empty envelope, right there and then.

"Wen!" Mom exclaims, looking at my messy working-out in dismay as I scrub out numbers and move things around, poking holes in the flimsy paper with my pen. "You're going to be *late*."

Thinking fast, I finish the thing with a messy flourish and shove the empty envelope back under the door. Miss Spencer can put today's work in a new one; she's got plenty.

Again, I've left off the remainder. It's me giving Henry an extra annoying poke in the ribs. I'm trying to get a reaction. Something more from him than a circle drawn in red pencil.

"Let's see how he likes *that!*" I tell Mom triumphantly as we start walking again towards school.

"Maybe they still had something left over, from Monday, to eat." Mom's voice is hopeful as we walk towards school. "It was quite a big serving, the Monday serving, and I'll have money to buy groceries again by Friday, when your father gets paid. We can make the food we have last until then, Wen, if we make a big pot of congee for tonight, and tomorrow."

I think about the single piece of pork belly defrosting in the fridge on a plate, and sigh. Congee, this savory porridge you make out of rice and stock and whatever meat and dried food you have handy—like black mushrooms, preserved Chinese pork sausage, pickled vegetables or fried shallots—is *not* my favorite food. It's too gloopy. And a bit tasteless. But Mom gets her housekeeping money on Friday with the start of the new month, so congee it will have to be for the next two days. For Mom and me, *and* Henry and his dad.

Hope they like it more than I do.

"Make it a *big* pot," I tell Mom as she leaves me at the school gate. "Use *lots* of rice and stock. And give Henry and his dad all the meat."

Mom squeezes my arm. "You have a good heart,

Wen." She's dressed in her lilac wool suit today, with uncomfortable-looking square-toed high-heeled dark-brown shoes with a dark-brown handbag to match. I think how her narrow feet must always hurt, the toes always pushed together into points.

"So do you, Mom." I give her arm a return squeeze, trying to imagine what she does all day while she waits for me that isn't some variation on cooking, cleaning, fetching or mending. While she walks away, her back very straight, her long, beautiful hair swinging, I wonder what she thinks of, what she dreams, once the shopping, cleaning, chopping and cooking are done.

At 3:42 p.m. exactly, we enter Mrs. Xenakis's pharmacy. Mr. and Mrs. Wu are already waiting for us, dressed like Mom is in their best clothes, even though all they're doing is getting their injections done.

Mr. Wu is in another dusty-looking three-piece suit, this time a navy pinstripe. Mrs. Wu is wearing black silky pants, black silk slippers and a high-collared, long-sleeved blouse in a silky grey floral fabric with pearl buttons, her chin-length bob combed very neatly and secured on each side by a jeweled hair slide. They both look anxious, but their wrinkled faces relax when they see Mom walk in.

Mrs. Xenakis explains each of the steps to Mom in English, and Mom translates them into Shanghainese. The elderly couple nod to show that they understand, with Mr. Wu offering to go first. He takes off his navy suit jacket and carefully places it over the back of the fold-out plastic chair that he is directed to sit on, rolling up his left shirt sleeve and exposing a sticklike, wrinkly arm. His stoic expression doesn't change at all as Mrs. Xenakis gives him his flu shot, his hollow-cheeked face breaking into laughter lines when Mrs. Xenakis urges him to take a lollipop or a small bag of licorice allsorts afterwards, from the big glass jar full of treats.

Clutching a bright bag of licorice cubes, Mr. Wu stands and helps his wife into the seat. Mrs. Wu, her expression pinched and frightened, reaches for Mom's hand, grasping it tightly as the needle goes into the papery skin of her right arm. Mom helps Mrs. Wu fold back down the sleeve of her thin blouse after Mrs. Xenakis is finished, buttoning the cuff gently. The old lady pats the back of Mom's hand as she takes a red lollipop. I giggle as she rips off the plastic covering immediately and sticks it into her mouth, smiling like a little kid.

Mrs. Xenakis turns to Mom gratefully. "I have a lot of older Chinese customers," she says. "And it's always very difficult for me to make them understand what I'm doing, or to feel less frightened. You're a godsend, Mrs. Zhou. Thank you."

"Call me Teresa," Mom replies in her careful English, which I still find weird to listen to; her voice is familiar, but also unfamiliar at the same time. "Mrs. Zhou is my husband's mother."

I look at Mom, gobsmacked. Dad never let me pick an English name to use at school, even though I begged because no one was saying "Wen" (kinda rhymes with "urn," but shorter) properly. Everyone had been calling me "When," and some kids still do. Whenever I asked, Dad would say something cheery like *The name I gave you is the name you're taking to the grave!* and that was that.

But Mom, whom I know as Mei Ling, has gone and picked Teresa for herself, and I wonder if she got it out of a Chinese celebrity magazine, or off the TV. I kind of . . . like it. I think.

Mom grins, suddenly, which makes her look much younger. "My husband's mother is a very frightening woman who lives in Beijing. We do not get along. We do not see"—Mom wrinkles up her face, concentrating hard on getting the phrase right—"eye to eye."

Mrs. Xenakis laughs. "I know a bit about that, being a childless 'career woman' who cannot cook! Could you please tell Mr. and Mrs. Wu to wait fifteen minutes before they go home?"

Mom translates Mrs. Xenakis's words into Shanghainese. Her expression changes when she sees the time on her watch: 4:09 p.m. The small, quick favor has taken longer than either of us expected.

"Wen?" she says breathlessly. "I'm sorry, Mrs. Xenakis, but Wen and I must go—we are late."

Mom explains to the Wus that we are expected at home, and we practically run out of the shop, arriving home as the phone is ringing, possibly for the second or third time.

Mom's *"Wéi?"* sounds strained and unnatural. She's puffed from running for the telephone as I lock the front door before trailing into the kitchen.

"Why was I running?" Mom says into the mouthpiece, looking at me. "Wen needed help with something in her bedroom. No, she's fine," she adds hurriedly. "We're both fine. No, there's nothing wrong."

After Mom hangs up, she sits at the kitchen table with me for a while, watching me finish a project on bacteria. "It needs a picture," Mom says suddenly. "There." She points at an empty spot in the lower left-hand corner.

She's right. My piece of poster paper is a wall of boring words. Everything is always better with a picture.

I get a green pencil and a red pencil out of my pencil case and draw a cell in green with an arrow coming out of it, the same cell splitting with two more arrows coming out of each half, and then two separate cells. I invite Mom to pick up the red pencil, which she does expectantly, and instruct her to draw two sets of red squiggles in each blob, representing a nucleus and a bunch of chromosomes, pointing to the places in the diagram where they are needed. She does so with relish, and we look down on our picture with satisfaction.

Mom raises an eyebrow at me in enquiry. "Good?" she says in English.

"Binary fission!" I tell her proudly, giving her two thumbs up.

Mom pulls the paper closer, studying the picture we've drawn together. "I wish I could do that," she replies wistfully in Chinese. "Be in two places at once. Then four. Then everywhere. Taking up all the space."

She tucks a bit of my hair behind my ear. Then she gets up to heat the pork and mushroom congee she made earlier in the day, ladling it into bowls for her and me, and filling a large thermos for Henry and his dad.

"Eat quickly," Mom says. "I want to drop it off and be home before it gets too dark." She rubs her arms. "I've just had this strange feeling all day. Something sitting heavily in my chest."

When I open my mouth to ask if she's all right, she cuts me off. "It's just nonsense. A silly feeling. But let's be quick, okay?"

While Mom is washing our dinner bowls and carefully storing the pot of remaining congee in the fridge for tomorrow's dinner, I get my colored pencils back out and draw Henry a quick cartoon of an airplane, with him in it, circling the world with *Not too long to go!* in a banner across the bottom. Then I stick it to the side of the thermos.

Henry hasn't been outside his house for almost two weeks now. I wonder if he and his dad have even spoken to each other properly in all that time, and if his dad ever listens to what he's saying—really listens—or is just a walking, ranty lecture on two legs, like my dad. Those competitions that say *The judges' decision is final. No correspondence will be entered into* sum up my dad perfectly.

I also wonder if Henry's dad is made of disappointment like my dad is—at Henry, at the way life turned out.

The air is very cold as we turn the corner with the big thermos. The wind picks up the picture of Henry in the airplane, making it flutter against my hand as we pass Mrs. Xenakis locking up the darkened pharmacy for the night.

"Thanks again, Mrs., uh, Teresa," she says, touching Mom on the sleeve. "For today. It was very kind, what you did, volunteering your time like that."

Mrs. Xenakis is not wearing her white lab coat anymore, and is in a skirt suit and high-heeled shoes, just like Mom is. It's lady armor, I realize suddenly. Not the most comfortable or practical kind. But clothes to face down the world in, nevertheless. Just for a second, it makes sense why Mom doggedly continues to do what she does—tries to save even those suits where the holes threaten to overwhelm what fabric is left. What would she be without them? Throwing even one of them away would be like throwing away some part of herself.

Mom inclines her head, embarrassed, and we move to walk on, but Mrs. Xenakis tightens her grip on Mom's jacket sleeve. "I was just wondering, if your schedule isn't too busy . . ."

Mrs. Xenakis stops, as if she's fishing around for the right words.

Mom looks surprised, and I am too. Mrs. Xenakis always knows what to say. She has to talk to people all day. She's never lost for words, like she is now.

That's Mom all the time; sometimes it's even me— when I'm talking to Mom and can't find the right word to use in Chinese so I have to stick an English word into the middle of a mostly Chinese sentence—but it's never Mrs. X.

"Yes?" Mom's tone is enquiring, once the silence drags out a little too long.

We all look down at the battered thermos in Mom's hands and Mrs. Xenakis says with a rush, "I've noticed that you're very good, you know, with Henry, and the Wus. I think you'd be a great asset to me, and to the doctor who works next door, during the day."

Mom and I look at Mrs. Xenakis, mystified.

"I'm offering you a job, Mrs. . . . Teresa . . ." Mrs. Xenakis explains in a rush. "Well, me and Dr. Gupta are. We talked about it just this morning, in fact, when I said you were coming in to help out in the afternoon. Just a few hours a day, maybe one or two days a week to start with? We'll schedule all the doctor's appointments for the old people on those days, so that you can be available to translate, if we need you to. I can put up a sign in the window, in English and Chinese—you can help me do that, if you like? Something that says you'll be here, to talk to, to help. Just like you're doing right now." Mrs. Xenakis nods at the thermos in Mom's hands. "It might involve you ducking in and out between my place and the clinic, but you'd soon get the hang of it."

I understand maybe a beat before Mom does. "That's

great, Mrs. X!" I exclaim, pinching Mom's sleeve and giving her arm a shake. "Mā!" I say in Mandarin, because Mom hasn't said a word in reply, she's too shocked. "She wants you to work in the pharmacy, and that clinic." I point out the two darkened buildings sitting side by side. "Isn't that *great*? They're just around the corner from home. It's perfect. You could earn a bit of money. Not be by yourself all day."

I think of Fay Xiao, frozen in her chair in a dark house. Cut off from everyone, from life outside.

Mom shakes her head finally. "I'm sorry, Mrs. Xenakis." She stumbles over the pharmacist's surname. "I don't think I can."

"He won't even know!" I insist hotly. "And it will get you out of the house."

"I'm out of the house *now*," Mom hisses at me in Chinese, distressed. "And I would like to get back to the house before it gets too dark. You heard what he said yesterday. We should not even be doing this, Wen. It is asking too much. I *can't*."

Mrs. Xenakis takes a step back at the look on Mom's face, the sound of Mom's voice. Even though she can't understand a word of what Mom's just said, she's heard and seen *the fear.*

Con Xenakis tells us proudly at school that his aunt chases shoplifters clear down the street and deals with drunk people and violent people all the time on her own. Maybe Mrs. Xenakis doesn't understand Mom's terror, but even she recognizes it.

"Will you just think about it?" Mrs. Xenakis tells Mom hastily now. "No pressure, Teresa, but we could really use you around here. We'll pay in advance for the week to help you get started, see how you find it. You can start right away—tomorrow, in fact. And stop any time, no questions asked. Dr. Gupta, she's the GP next door," Mrs. Xenakis explains, "she says all the time that we badly need help. Says she's no good at charades, that there must be a better way to go about doing things. I can speak to your husband, if you'd like . . . ?"

I think about how silly that sounds. That Mom needs Dad's permission—as if a part-time job with Mrs. Xenakis is something like a school excursion form that Dad has to sign. After the last school excursion form he signed, I almost died. The school told my parents I fell in the water and *had a bit of a shock,* but to this day, he still has no idea I was carried out to sea so far that I almost drowned.

Mom shakes her head violently, her sleek hair falling around her face.

"We'll think about it, Mrs. X," I say quickly. "Thanks."

I pull Mom away up the street as Mrs. Xenakis lifts one hand hesitantly in farewell and unlocks her car, staring up the road after us.

"We need to get home," Mom says in Chinese, her

voice very tight and anxious. "We shouldn't be doing this. Someone will see us. Someone will talk. We've done too much already."

I ring the doorbell at Henry's house quickly twice, leaving the thermos on the doormat, right at the base of the security door. The cartoon airplane is facing inwards, so that it will be the first thing Henry sees. To remind him that he needs to be strong enough to step outside, to step into the cockpit of the airplane he'll build one day and be ready to *go*.

I push down the thought that maybe, one day, I won't be ready myself. That I will need someone's permission to do things, just like Mom does, for the rest of my life, even when I'm old. Losing the ability, by slow degrees, to decide for myself: what I want to wear, what I want to eat, what I want to think, how I want to *be*. The thought makes me shudder.

I can't let that happen to me. I won't.

Even though it's not quite dark yet, Mom and I walk twice as fast home today, this nameless dread hanging over the two of us. Mom's right hand is placed flat over her heart the whole way. When we reach the front of the pharmacy, Mom actually puts her arm through mine and pulls me in closer, leaning on me, as if she's very cold or very tired, or very old.

When we turn the corner and see our house, Mom

and I actually stop and hug each other tight because our driveway isn't empty like it usually is.

I have to remind myself: It's *Wednesday*. Not Tuesday.

But Dad's old, immaculately maintained navy blue Toyota is in the carport. It's not even eight p.m.— the dinner rush is happening right now, over two kilometers away, without Dad.

Something bad must have happened at the restaurant.

CHAPTER 9

DANGER

WHEN WE SCRAMBLE INSIDE THE HOUSE, DAD'S sitting in front of the TV, watching the evening news. Even though we're making loads of noise, he doesn't look around when we pass the doorway to the lounge room, on the way to the kitchen. He just sits there like a stone, unmoving, still wearing his suit and tie and shoes. The glow of the TV is flickering over his face because he hasn't bothered to turn on the light and the room is dark.

It's something Fay Xiao would have done, and my skin tightens in alarm.

I think of all the times when Dad hasn't been able to get out of bed. When life must feel so worthless to him that he doesn't speak to anyone, or look at anyone, he just withdraws while Mom keeps the whole house ticking over until he decides to emerge again.

I don't know what's worse—him shouting at us with his face all twisted up and dark with fury, or him immobile and unreachable behind a closed bedroom door or in front of a flickering TV in the dark. It feels like there's never any in-between. I can't breathe.

Mom and I look at each other anxiously as she shrugs off her brown suit jacket and puts on her black apron. "Go and ask him if he wants any soup," she tells me urgently. The same soup Mom used as a base for the thermos of congee we just left at Henry's house.

Congee and soup is pretty much all we have left in the house to eat. If Dad wants eight dishes tonight, we're in real trouble.

"Could *you* ask him?" I beg, thankful we came home empty-handed, with nothing to explain.

Mom gives me a hard look and hurries out. For several minutes, I hear her voice, sharp and enquiring, but I don't hear Dad's.

"What's *wrong* with you?" she finally shouts in frustration. "It's like speaking to a statue when you're like this!"

I go very still. Mom never yells at Dad. She's never dared.

She comes back into the kitchen, and I see it before

she does. My eyes widen in warning at how Dad jumps out of his chair and runs at her, pulling her around by one arm so that her long hair flies out behind her, and she cries out in pain and alarm.

"What's wrong with *you*?" he roars. "With *her*?"

He points at me with a shaking finger, and I go hot, my whole face flushing from my neck to my hairline with fear. What is it that I've done? This is Dad when he's in a mood to burn things.

He screams, "I *forbade* you to have anything to do with those people, and you defied me!"

Our eyes, Mom's and mine, fly to each other across the kitchen. How does he *know*?

"I *saw* you," Dad shouts, as if I've just spoken the question out loud. "I saw you leaving something at the house of that disgraced man. A man who is not your husband. A man I told you to stay away from!"

He shakes Mom hard by the arm and I yell, "Stop it! It was my fault! I *made* Mom do it. She didn't want to do it. I forced her to help me, to help Henry."

Dad turns on me, his grip so tight on Mom's arm that his knuckles are white. "Who is the adult here? You or her? This is *her* fault. The fact that you are a stupid, lying, disobedient girl is your mother's fault. *Who* is with you all day? *Who* has made you into this useless, insolent child? *She* has."

Actually, you have, I think, too afraid to say the words out loud. *You've made us this way. Having to sneak around just to get the things that should be done, things that are good and right, done in peace.*

"Jin, please," Mom pleads, twisting in his grip. "We won't do it again. Forget about it. It's not important."

"Mom," I insist loudly, "it *is* important. Dad's always talking about *benevolence* and what it means to be good, to be cultured, to be worthwhile. He gave me a *boy's* name, remember? *Cultured strength.* Being cultured and being benevolent and being strong can't just mean that we only help ourselves while other people are suffering and we can do something about it! It can't just mean that we serve our parents while we ignore all the other people who need our help."

Dad drops Mom's arm and turns to face me, gripping the back of one of the kitchen chairs.

"Why are you talking *back?*" he roars. "Who gave you the right to speak to me like this? We cannot be connected to people like them. I *saw* you," Dad repeats. "I was driving home and I *saw you.* I could not believe my eyes, that you are living here in this house and openly disobeying my rules. It is complete chaos, disorder, everything is upside down, you are a *child* . . ."

Dad's voice cracks and Mom and I look at each other in horror when he gobbles, "They fired me! *Me!* An educated man. They sent me home! And then I *saw* you . . ."

"What have you *done*, Jin?" Mom breathes. Her eyes fly to the fridge, which she and I both know to be practically empty except for a few slices of bread and ham. Friday is payday. It's still two days away. The first of the month is always payday.

Until maybe it isn't.

I take a step closer to Mom, who's rubbing her arm absently, her eyes fixed on Dad.

Dad is breathing very hard as he leans on the back of the kitchen chair, and I wonder whether the two spheres of his life have finally met and crashed together. The man he is at home—unpredictable, unreasonable, controlling, hot-tempered—and the man he's supposed to be at work, where nothing can ever be too much trouble—icy, remote, but polite in the face of every indignity, every customer's whim, no matter how ridiculous. *(Can I have the sweet and sour sauce in a little jug on the side? I asked for three types of chili sauce and you only brought me two? Does it come with zucchini? Can you take the zucchini out, because I hate zucchini and it makes me cry?)*

Dad looks up at us now with red eyes. "The man *deserved* it!" he spits. "The whole table was full of drunk white men, rude, racist, unbearable—but he was the worst! When he called me an *uppity little Chink* . . ."

I gasp out loud and Mom takes a step backwards, towards me.

". . . I tipped an entire plate of Cantonese beef over him. The owner told me to leave at once."

"*Jin!*" Mom's voice is hushed as Dad makes a harsh barking sound, like a sob.

I'm not really thinking when I mutter out loud, "What are we going to do *now*?"

Dad raises his head higher and draws the chair out from under the table, shakes it at me.

"*We*," he snarls, "are going to give our parents no further cause for anxiety. *We* are going to obey without question. *We* are going to stop making a spectacle of ourselves by aiding the family of a disgraceful suicide!"

"And what happens if we don't?" I regret my words as soon as they tumble out, but I plunge on anyway. "What if we don't stop helping because it's up to *us*"— my eyes fly to Mom's, beseechingly, for backup—"to get Henry well enough and strong enough to sit an entrance exam this Saturday? An exam that *I* am also sitting for, so that I can learn enough, and be enough, to one day take care of myself and my family so that the fridge will be full of everything we need, when we need it?"

I know that by saying what I'm actually thinking for once, I've said too much.

Something in Dad's face shifts.

For a second, there's so much rage in it that he doesn't look human. He lifts the chair he's holding even higher and cracks it onto the floor so hard that one of the wooden legs splinters through the middle. Mom and I jump.

The leg is hanging at a funny angle as Dad points what's left of the chair at me. "You *stop*—you stop right now doing what you're doing, or you can get out of this house."

"Wen!" Mom breathes. "Just go to your room. *Please.* I'll talk to him, he doesn't mean it."

But Dad does mean it, because he roars, "Don't like it? Don't like my rules? Then just get out of my house!"

"Jin!" Mom's voice is high and frightened. "How can you say this? She's a *child.* She's your *daughter.*"

Dad turns his red eyes on Mom and doesn't reply, because he doesn't have to.

If I were a boy, life would be different. Life would undoubtedly be better. The universe would be in perfect balance. I wouldn't be a walking daily reminder of something missing, some kind of *lack.*

But I'm not a boy. And I can change that as much as I can change where my heart lies beating inside my chest. Which is exactly not at all.

My voice sounds small and funny as I remind Dad, "Tzu-Chang asked the master about what makes a benevolent man. There are *five* things . . ."

I search my memory quickly for one of Dad's interminable lectures. They are all there, filed away, because I may be bad at maths, but I have a memory like an elephant for words.

"One is *respectfulness*," I continue breathlessly. "The second is *tolerance*. The third is *trustworthiness*. The fourth is *quickness*. The last is *generosity*. If a man is respectful, he will not be met with rudeness. If a man is tolerant, he will win people over. If a man is trustworthy, he will be given responsibility. If he is quick, he will achieve results. If he is generous, he will be put in a position over all others."

Dad's face is so mottled, so still, that I have to resist the desperate and immediate urge to run far, far away.

"I'm trying, Dad," I say quietly, moving around him so that I'm standing near the doorway to the front hall, fighting the overwhelming feeling of wanting to hide. "Mom's trying. We are both trying to be *good men*. We have always tried, every day, every moment we are awake. Now it's *your* turn."

"Wen!" Mom whispers.

I know I've passed the point of no return. I feel like I've lost my footing and a riptide is sweeping me out and I'm losing sight of the land. I *know* that feeling. The sound of the waves pounding down on my head, how there is no longer any air to breathe, no light, and the only element left is one that can kill you.

I can either swim now, or I can drown.

I hold up my hand to stop Mom saying anything else. The way we are is more than a little bit my mother's fault. For not ever pushing back. For allowing our "permitted" boundaries—hers *and* mine—to get so small. It's true.

I'm a kid. It shouldn't be up to me to always be pointing out the things that don't make sense, that aren't fair, that aren't *right*.

Dad's eyes are very bright and hard as he snarls, "What makes *you* a better *man* than your own father?"

He throws the chair down, and it falls on its side as Mom and I flinch. "That entrance exam? They will laugh at you, they will laugh at Henry, like they laughed at me! What makes you better than me?" He scoffs again. "What makes you think you can pass when your own father can't pass? Why bother? It will end in *nothing*."

"Something always comes from nothing," I retort, and there's a shift in Mom's pinched, white features as she recognizes the words that she once told me, the words of the ancient philosopher Lao Tzu, which I've never forgotten either. "Miss Spencer and Henry think I'm good enough to at least try. I haven't given up on trying yet. If they laugh at me, and it ends in nothing? I will try something else. *I will never stop trying*."

Dad rears back, pointing a shaking finger at me. "For people like *you*," he spits, "life will break your heart. Over and over. Unless you get wise, unless you get *smart*."

"Still," I say, backing away from the light of the kitchen, from the two of them standing, framed, in the doorway, receding in my sight. "I don't want to end up like you—smaller and meaner than you should be."

"You're a *child*," Dad reminds me again shakily, as if I don't recognize that fact every waking moment of every day. "You *must* obey me under the law. I forbid you to help Henry Xiao, and I forbid you to sit that exam."

"It doesn't matter," I say, more bravely than I'm feeling, "because in this country, the real laws protect even the children. Miss Spencer will help me do what it takes to sit the exam. Even if it means I have to leave home to do it, and live somewhere else."

Mom gasps and puts her hands over her mouth.

Dad is still roaring "You can't do it! You're not good enough!" as I walk out the front door, still wearing my school uniform and the slippers I'm only ever supposed to wear inside the house.

I'm on autopilot as I storm towards the corner where the shops are, my floppy indoor slippers tripping me up with every step.

Instead of turning left to go towards Henry's house and my school, I go right towards the scout hall, where Nikki Kuol is going to have her big birthday party on Sunday—the one that I'm not allowed to go to, but long to attend so fiercely, it's like a pain in my body.

No, you can't do it.

No, you aren't good enough.

No, no, no, no, *no.*

I sit outside the scout hall for a while, on the steps. Everything is dark now. There's no one around, and it feels like nothing in my life will ever change. I will always be caught up between *the rage* and *the fear* and it will never get any better than this.

For a second, I wonder if being caught in that gap was too much for Henry's mother. And just for a second, I think I understand why she did it, and feel so much sadness that tears spill down my cheeks in the darkness.

After that, I lose track of time as I walk around the neighborhood aimlessly, dashing away the tears that keep running down my face. It's when I hear the sound of a stone being kicked off the footpath behind me that I realize I'm not alone.

Two men are walking behind me, talking quietly. I

don't know how long they've been there and, instantly, every hair on my body seems to stand up in warning.

I cross the street quickly, almost falling out of my house slippers, and they cross too. I start heading back in the direction of the scout hall, and their voices seem to grow louder, their footsteps faster, as if they're trying to catch up with me.

They will eventually, I know they will; I can't run properly in these slippers.

I cross again, taking a diagonal path towards Mrs. Xenakis's pharmacy, and they cross as well. They're now only a hundred or so meters behind me as I pass the local shops. A scream rising inside me, I cross another street, and this time I hear laughter, very close. For them, it's a game. I'm not sure what that game means for me and don't want to find out.

Half running now, as fast as my slippers will let me, I head towards the pedestrian bridge that leads to Henry's house and hear their footsteps pick up even more quickly behind me.

Maybe Dad was right. Maybe it's always too dangerous to leave home for people like me. There are so many stairs ahead! They might catch me on the stairs. I might trip and fall. I don't know what I'm going to do.

It's late, so there's less traffic than during the day. I make the split-second decision to rip my slippers off and run straight across the road, six lanes wide, in my

socked feet through the steady traffic that's still passing up and down in front of the Xiaos' place. Someone
honks at me loudly as I run, the sound of an engine
brake shuddering nearby almost scaring me out of my
skin. Out of the corner of my eye, a light-colored hatch-
back swerves to avoid me. Mom walks me to and from
school every day just so that I don't ever do anything
like this—dodge between the cars and trucks, taking
my life in my hands just to save a few extra meters. But
I'm terrified.

Should I go for the doorbell or just bang on the windows of Henry's house when I reach it? What if they
don't hear? What if they don't let me in? What if something really bad does happen to me, and no one ever
finds me, and that's it—one life, this life, finished and
done and over?

The breath is sobbing in my lungs and throat as I
throw myself up the footpath at Henry's place, desper-
ately mashing the doorbell beside his front door with
my thumb.

The two men are right there, standing at the very
edge of the Xiaos' front yard, talking and laughing and
watching. But they turn and skulk off finally when
someone throws open the wooden door and light
streams out onto the front porch from the inside.

I blink through my tears at the light, refracted like
rainbows in my vision.

"Wen?" Mr. Xiao says in surprise through the screen door. "It's late! What has happened?"

He's too polite to mention that I appear to be standing on his doorstep in my uniform and socks, with no shoes on.

I see the silhouette of Mr. Xiao's head peering from left to right, looking for my mother, my father.

He starts unlocking the wire door and I say tiredly, "Please, if it's all right, I'll just sit here for a while, Mr. Xiao? I don't want to come in. I was just being followed, and I didn't feel safe. I'm sorry about the congee we left you before, how tasteless and measly the serving was. I'm sorry to trouble you."

I collapse on the front step with my back to the security door, resting my sweating, teary face in my hands. I don't think I've ever felt so scared in my life. Not even when Dad broke that chair in front of us just now.

I had a context for a broken chair. But not for being followed by two men in the dark.

"If you're sure, Wen?" Mr. Xiao's voice is worried. "I'll just leave the front door open so that you can call out, if you need anything . . ."

I feel him hovering there for a moment more, behind the locked screen door, unsure what to do about me sitting on the doorstep in my school uniform and socks at 10:04 p.m.

At 10:11 p.m., just when my heart's slowing enough

that I'm thinking of sprinting home, I hear someone sit down heavily on the floor on the other side of the wire door.

Senses on high alert, I stay there with my back to him, and we sit, not talking, just breathing the same air companionably, until I start talking, all of it spilling out. About Dad losing his job, the fight, Nikki's party, the men sniggering and following and getting closer and closer in the dark. At some stage I find I'm crying again, tears sliding down my cheeks, and I'm glad Henry can't see me.

"But enough about me," I say finally, smearing the back of my hand across my face. I've said too much. I should be letting Henry talk.

There's a long silence. I can almost hear Henry's brain grinding slowly into gear, telling him, *This is where you are expected to say something in return. In English. She wants you to practice your English.*

"Actually, you don't have to say anything," I say hastily. "You don't have to say or do anything at all."

But in a voice that sounds strange and rusty, as if from disuse, Henry declares, "To live is to risk everything!"

My cheeks are still damp with tears, but it makes both of us laugh, unexpectedly, to hear Henry channelling Mr. Cornish, with his twirly mustache.

"Only on Wednesdays," I reply tiredly. "Wednesdays, when your father loses his job."

"On Wednesdays, when your father loses his job," Henry says carefully in English, "there is no 'happy medium.'"

"You're so ready for that exam," I murmur back.

"So are you," Henry says hesitantly, still speaking in English. "See you on Saturday."

As I'm about to turn out of the front of Henry's place, I look back quickly to see the light streaming around his seated figure silhouetted behind the wire, facing me.

The silhouette raises its right hand slowly in a victory fist.

I'm still smiling as the shadow of Henry Xiao is lost to sight.

He's still not *outside*, I think, but it's a start.

CHAPTER 10

EVERYTHING CHANGES

Yīqiè dōu gǎibiàn

WHEN I REACH HOME, THE LIGHT BY OUR FRONT door is on as if it's been left on for Dad. But I know that it's on for me this time. I'm the one who's come home late. I'm the one who's gone out in my lady armor and house slippers to battle devils and ghosts, and lived to tell the tale.

Mom quietly opens the security door before I can even place my hand on it. Her eyes are wet with tears.

I don't apologize. I just say simply, "I did exactly what Dad told me to do—got out of the house. I was being obedient, for a change. Did he burn anything while I was away?"

Mom's laugh sounds like a sob.

I don't tell her about the men, or about running

across the main road through all the cars in my socks, weeping in fear, with my heart squeezed up high in my throat.

And Mom doesn't ask anything. She just pulls me in and gives me a fierce hug.

For a moment, I stand there frozen. She doesn't usually do more than pat me vaguely on the top of one shoulder, or an arm. We aren't huggers.

Then I hug her back.

It feels good, but also super awkward. Needing practice.

The two of us are tangled in her hair for a long time before she whispers, "Don't *ever* do that again! I even went out looking for you. I walked everywhere, up and down all the streets—even to Henry's house—but I couldn't find you anywhere."

I think about the two of us missing each other out there, in the badly lit streets, and what might have happened if those two men had followed my beautiful mother walking alone in her prim suit and silly high-heeled shoes, instead of me in my school uniform and slippers, and I go cold.

Mom lets go of me and locks the front door. We walk very quietly past the closed door to my parents' bedroom and I imagine Dad in there, wide awake in the dark and seething with bitter thoughts. I'm grateful, but scared at the same time, that there's no noise coming from behind the door.

Do I prefer it when Dad is roaring? Or catatonic? And will there ever be an Option C?

Maybe not. I need to stop hoping for an Option C, because it's not up to me—it's up to him. I just need to stop feeling angry and disappointed that this is how it is, and keep moving, keep learning, keep drawing, keep writing, keep running—with slippers or without.

Mom watches me brush my teeth, and pulls the quilt cover over me after I change into my pajamas and get into bed. She sits down on the edge of the mattress, the hallway light putting her face in shadow as she looks down at me.

Something feels different, but I'm so tired I just close my eyes and go to sleep with her still sitting there, watching me as if I might vanish in a puff of smoke.

In the morning, the house is still very quiet as Mom hands me my plastic lunchbox with a single ham sandwich in it. On days like these, where Dad's in his cave and won't come out, we always talk in whispers; we're on tenterhooks. Everything's normal on top—the duck sailing smoothly over the pond—but underneath, everything is churning. We're very good at pretending.

Mom's dressed today in her favorite light-blue skirt suit, with a crisp white shirt underneath. She looks as fresh and pretty as one of those fancy jewelry boxes that diamond rings come in, from that expensive store they named the movie after. The advertisements are always on the buses that go past my school, but the store's nowhere near here, and probably never will be.

I tell Mom about how good she looks, and she smiles before bending and digging around in the wooden chest we keep shoes in, in the hallway. "Help me find the tan pair of heels," she murmurs, sweeping her long, straight hair over one shoulder to keep it out of the way as she searches.

I wrinkle my nose. "The tan ones don't go with what you're wearing," I say as we dig around below pairs and pairs of Dad's worn-out black business shoes and multiple pairs of cartoon-character slippers—indoor and outdoor—that I've long outgrown, and that should have been thrown away.

Mom makes a small sound, then pulls out the pair of shoes she's been looking for.

The tan shoes are wedge-heeled and open-toed, clunky and ugly and worn-out looking, but she slips her feet into them with a satisfied expression.

"They *are* terrible"—she grins, looking down—"but they have the lowest heel out of every pair I own. And I'm going to be doing a lot of walking today."

As I step outside the door, Mom mutters something under her breath and runs back inside our silent house. A minute later she's back, locking the door from the outside and dropping the bunch of house keys into the blue, white and red–striped tote bag she's carrying— one of the tough, ugly ones you get from a Chinese grocery store with a zip that always breaks in two seconds but with a body that lasts forever and will probably take longer than nuclear waste to break down.

I stare at it in wonder. "That's the bag you take food shopping, Mom! It doesn't match what you're wearing *at all*."

I wave my hand at her, taking in the stripy bag, the pristine blue skirt suit and the horrible tan shoes. "None of it does!" Mom's outfits *always* match.

I don't remind her that we have no money for her to go food shopping, and probably have no money at all now that Dad's been fired, because she seems . . . happy.

"I'm going for practicality over style today," Mom replies in Chinese. "Hurry, Wen. We have a lot to do."

I wonder what she means. It's just a normal day, except that Dad's *home*, possibly forever, and will probably never come out of his bedroom again.

When we reach Henry's house there's the usual completed homework in the new envelope that Miss Spencer gave me yesterday before the bell went for home-time. But underneath it is the crinkly envelope with the longest long division question in the world on it and my handwritten answer. But there's something new, drawn in thick black pen, curled up under the equation that Henry and I put together.

I start laughing as I study it, and Mom does too. Henry's circled my one deliberate error as usual, but he's also done something else, and I feel a spark of hope.

I drop my backpack at my feet and hunt around in the front pocket for a pen, dragging my fingernails through the drifts of pencil shavings and paper clips, rubber bands, crumbs and Band-Aid wrappers that have collected in the corners, until I find a biro.

"Wen," Mom says in warning, looking at her watch. She seems sharper today. More focused. Impatient.

Hastily, I scribble beside the angry dragon:

I never forget the remainder.
The remainder is the most important part,
Henry Xiao, because the whole wouldn't be
whole again without it!

Then I shove my note, and the angry dragon, back under Henry's door before Mom and I walk on.

"I think he's going to be okay," I say to Mom.

"I think so, too," Mom replies. "I just hope he's had something to eat since Tuesday! But we will fix that today."

I think of the almost empty packet of sliced ham left in the fridge, and the five slightly stale slices of bread, and wonder how.

I don't blame Nikki and Fatima for being a little cool towards me when I slide into the empty seat next to them after handing Miss Spencer Henry's latest packet of completed work. Fatima arranges the ends of her light-blue headscarf and looks down at the surface of her desk, while Nikki turns her head away, presenting me with a view of her glossy, unbound braids as she stares deliberately out the window.

"I'm really sorry," I say simply, because there's no time to explain the parameters, the dips and contours, of my life before the bell rings to start period one. Even being in the middle of it makes no sense to me—how the rules keep changing and expanding as I grow, but never ever in my favor. How would Nikki—whose cousin is an international skateboarder with a cool Korean girlfriend and who has an aunt that models for fashion designers in New York—understand why birthday parties, sleepovers, *fun*, are all things that are off limits? I can't even explain it to myself.

Nikki turns to me sharply, staring hard for a moment, and then something in her face softens. "*I get it*," she says, leaning forward. "It's different for us, too. It's so *unfair*. But I still wish you could come."

"So do I," I say fervently, blinking very fast to hold back tears. "But I'll be sending you good vibes from behind the walls of my house. You'll be able to *feel* them, the vibes will be so strong. You'll be begging for me to cut it out. *Begone, good vibes! Trouble me no further, this day!"*

Beside Nikki, Fatima laughs and shakes her head, the jeweled pin in her headscarf catching the fluorescent lighting from overhead.

"I'll save you a piece of cake." Nikki grins. "I'll just leave it on your doorstep after the party, ring the doorbell, then run away, fast, so that I don't get the door slammed in my face again!"

Miss Spencer hands me a new envelope of worksheets—some for me, plus the usual set for Henry—just before the end of the day. "This is it," she says as I pull my backpack out of my locker and dump it on the floor at my feet. "This is the last lot of extra homework. Tomorrow is Friday, and Saturday morning is the exam. You've both done more than enough. I'll just give you feedback on this lot sometime tomorrow, and then you're good to go, Wen."

"Am I really? Good to go?" I ask through my hair as I crouch and shove the envelope into my backpack. "Dad says I'm not good enough, that I can't do it and shouldn't even try."

Miss Spencer makes a low, snorting sound like an angry bull, and squats beside me.

"Do you actually believe that?" she asks. "Because if you do, then don't even bother."

"Excuse me, Miss," Billy Raum says, yanking his schoolbag out of his locker right over both our heads. He tries to get a look at what we're doing and I glare up at him so fiercely that he blinks and pulls his sharp, freckly nose right out of our business and backs away.

"No," I say slowly. "I think I have a chance, just like everyone else does, but I'm afraid." I jerk a thumb at Billy Raum's retreating back. "If I don't get in, everyone will know for real that I was kidding myself. Henry's a shoo-in, but me? For real? People will laugh, and I will probably never live it down. Dad will say it's my fault for *getting ideas*, and that I only have myself to blame, et cetera."

"What's the alternative?" Miss Spencer replies sternly. "Stay put? Don't try?"

After a moment, I nod in understanding.

I *know* what the alternative is. Not having the heart to get out of bed for days in a row, or get out of a sagging armchair in a cold, empty house that smells like mold and doesn't feel like a home because you refuse to treat it like one. Like the old Chinese saying goes, if you do it, you might die, sure. Doing something risky is on your head, and you have to bear the consequences. But what if you don't do it? You'll still die sometime—and the dying might be of an even worse kind. A slow kind of dying. Dying while you're living, by awful, incremental degrees.

"You're ready," Miss Spencer insists, jumping up and helping me to my feet. My bag is so heavy that I stagger sideways for a second after I swing it onto my back, and she has to steady me. "So is Henry. You show that school what *different* looks like, why different is important. Why they *need* you."

Miss Spencer walks me all the way to the front entrance and out onto the front steps.

At the distant gate, Mom is waiting in her usual place. She's looking around, shielding her eyes against the sun, but when she sees me and Miss Spencer standing under the archway entrance that has always looked to me like a frowny old mouth, she waves. Mom doesn't try to come inside the grounds—she never does, she wouldn't dream of it—but she looks Miss Spencer right in the eye and she smiles and keeps waving.

She's never done that before. Usually, Mom looks right through people because she's really shy, and worried about her English and that people might try to talk to her.

Surprised, Miss Spencer smiles and waves back.

When I walk closer, my eyes are drawn in astonishment to the bag Mom is holding, a plastic bag with three takeaway containers inside.

"Hurry, Wen," she says. "Before the food gets cold. I'm going to be too busy to cook for the next two days."

My eyes are drawn to the bag of takeaway food in astonishment. Mom *never* buys takeaway food. She always makes things from scratch from complicated recipes involving packets of dried foodstuffs and mounds of fresh meat and vegetables, and there's never any spare money for takeaway anyway. Whenever I need money for a school excursion, it takes her ages to fish little pockets of coins out of different jars and purses all over the house.

"Did you rob a takeaway shop?" I say incredulously as we bustle down the main road.

"Don't be silly, Wen," Mom says, then shocks me even more by turning in to the front gate of Henry's house, walking right up to the doorbell and ringing it twice, firmly.

"Uh," I say, remembering Dad screaming the words *disgraceful suicide* in my face.

We hear the usual shuffle of slippers approaching and the sound of two doors being unlocked. Mr. Xiao sticks his head outside cautiously, his somber face breaking into a smile as he catches sight of Mom in her duck-egg-blue suit and me with my packet of home-work for Henry.

I hand him the envelope, and Mom hands him the bag of food.

He looks down at it in surprise. The heavenly aroma is making me salivate.

Mom says in a rush of formal Chinese, "I did not make this, Mr. Xiao, and you have every right not to eat it and instead throw it directly away, but please ac-cept this poor substitute for a home-cooked meal . . ."

The expression on his face looks like the way my face feels. Utter confusion.

Mr. Xiao is still staring at the bag in his hand as he mumbles, "Henry is very lucky, Mrs. Zhou, to have such good friends."

"Henry is the good friend," Mom says firmly. "For giving Wen the courage to sit an exam she is entirely unprepared for."

"Hey!" I say in English, elbowing Mom. "Who says I'm . . ."

Mom elbows me back to tell me to *shut up* and I blink in surprise.

Henry's dad backs away from the door into the shadow of his house, clutching the loaded bag of food in one hand and the envelope of homework in the other. He doesn't appear to have heard a word that Mom was saying as he adds tearfully, "Friends that more than make up for the tragedy of Henry having such inadequate parents."

Mom and I exchange a look of horror as the screen door is shut gently in our faces and locked from the inside.

Mr. Xiao says heavily through the wire door. "Henry and I will pick you up at seven-fifteen on Saturday morning, Wen."

"I'll wait for you outside my house," I confirm in Chinese.

Mom's effusive "Thank you, thank you, Mr. Xiao" is cut off as Henry's dad shuts the wooden door, sealing himself and Henry back inside.

CHAPTER 11

LEAVING, AND RETURNING

"WHY ARE YOU WALKING SO *FAST?*" I SAY, WRIN-
kling my nose, my backpack jabbing me painfully in one
hip. "What's going *on*, Mom?"

As we crossed the pedestrian bridge in front of
Henry's house to reach our own side of the neighborhood, Mom explained that the takeaway bag she'd just
given Mr. Xiao contained a big serving of rice ("Enough
for two days at least!") and a serving of silken tofu with
chicken, shallots and salted fish, together with a container of slow-braised beef and vegetables. My mouth is
still watering as we head away from the bridge towards
the local shops, Mom practically running in her ugly
tan wedge shoes.

Outside Mrs. Xenakis's pharmacy, Mom stops and

reaches inside the blue, red and white grocery bag on her shoulder and pulls out the house keys. She holds them out to me, and I take them for the second time in my life, my mouth open in surprise.

"Now you go home and start your homework, Wen. Put the rice on to boil if I'm not home by five-thirty so that we can eat at six-fifteen. There are a few things I need to get from the grocer before I get back."

I think of Dad, brooding in his bedroom behind a closed door. What will we say to each other if he comes out? Will it be shouty Dad today, or silent Dad? And how do I explain why Mom's not home? I'm not feeling at all creative today. He'll be able to work out that she's most definitely *not* in the toilet.

"Where are *you* going to be?" I exclaim. I close my fingers over the heavy set of keys in my palm. "Did Mrs. Wu collapse inside the pharmacy again?"

Mom laughs. "Mrs. Wu is not collapsed inside, although she did stop in to buy some lip gloss and collect a prescription for antibiotic cream for Mr. Wu, who has a bad cut on his leg. A gardening accident, she said."

"How do you know all this?" I say, and then *zing*, I get it. My insides feel like jelly.

If I'm right, this is big. This is *huge*.

"Are you . . . *working* here now? Did you accept that job Mrs. Xenakis offered you?"

I feel like squealing and jumping up and down.

Mom nods vigorously, and her face seems a little bit lit up from the inside.

"Mrs. Xenakis"—Mom stumbles, like she usually does over the Greek surname—"*Nina,* said I could start right away, when I explained about . . ." Her gaze goes unfocused for a moment before settling on me again. "She won't need me every day, but she promised that on days that I am working I can still walk you to and from school. Go home to get dinner prepared, if I need to. She's already paid me for today and tomorrow. She needs me to come back on Monday, to interpret for a family from Shenzhen."

Mom grasps my hands where they are cupped around the keys, tilts her head up slightly and looks straight into my eyes. "You don't have to explain anything to him," she says in Chinese. "You tell him to wait until I get home. I'm the adult, remember? *I* will explain."

When I let myself into the house, it's still silent and my parents' bedroom door is still closed. Dad's still in bed, brooding. I practice my violin in the kitchen with the sliding door shut because it's the farthest point from their bedroom, so if Dad's asleep it won't be loud enough to wake him up.

At 5:30 p.m., Mom's still not home, so I move the washed rice waiting in a claypot on the kitchen bench onto a burner to cook.

I almost leap out of my skin at 5:42 when Dad slides the door open. "Where is your mother?" he demands.

His face is creased from sleeping all day. He's wearing a terrible old dark-blue tracksuit that's sagging at the hem and at the collar.

"She's at the pharmacy," I reply, hearing the little tremor in my voice.

"What about dinner?" Dad growls.

I point at the stove. "It's already cooking."

He looks across at the covered bowls of chopped vegetables sitting on the kitchen bench, makes a sound in the back of his throat, then walks away down the hall and shuts himself inside his bedroom again.

At six on the dot, Mom flings herself through the door with her stripy shopping bag, now bulging. She unloads its contents into the fridge before strapping on her black apron, pulling out the wok and taking other small bowls of sliced meat and tofu from the fridge.

In minutes, dinner is ready—but there are only three dishes on the table.

"Uh," I say as I set the table with glasses, bowls and chopsticks.

Mom cuts me off with a steely look. "Any number but seven is *fine*. Go and call your father to eat."

I knock on the closed bedroom door.

I say, "Dinner?" like a question, as if I'm asking him *for* dinner, instead of telling him that it's ready.

As Mom and I are sitting down at the table to eat, Dad appears again in his rumpled sleep suit, with his rumpled face, his usually severe, neatly combed hair still standing on end from all the tossing and turning he's done.

His voice is very quiet. "Where have you *been* all day?"

"At the pharmacy," Mom replies, a little shakily. She is unable to quite meet his eyes as she places a serving of meat and vegetables on top of his bowl of rice. "Doing what I can . . . to help the family."

Dad still hasn't sat down. He just stands there looming over the two of us, his face twisted into a shadow of its usual sneer. "You can't speak English properly," he mutters. "You're not even educated. You would be an embarrassment to any workplace."

Mom and I exchange glances and I pray that she doesn't answer the way that I would: *What? The same way that you were?*

But the silence just hangs there uncomfortably after Dad's words.

The kitchen is still hot and airless from all the flash-frying and steaming Mom's done. I don't know if I should start eating, or instead, run and snatch up the back door key that's hanging on a small hook inside the pantry and let myself out into the night. I know what I want to do.

I don't want to be here. I can't stand it anymore.

When I grow up, I don't want to be like her, or like him. I'm going to answer to *me*.

I half rise out of my seat to maybe run again, and Mom's voice, quiet but stern, stops me. "Wen?" she says. "Sit."

Dad circles the table. "There's not enough *food*," he snarls.

"It's not *Tuesday*," Mom says softly, picking up her chopsticks and putting a slice of meat into her mouth. She doesn't remind him that tomorrow is Friday. The day he was supposed to get paid and give her money to buy groceries with.

Dad stops prowling and I find that I've clenched my fists on the tabletop, ready to defend myself from a random clip across the ears, or maybe a porcelain bowl full of food thrown in my face.

If the air could crackle any more with this unspoken *something*, I think I'd be able to hear it.

It's like a scene from a dream as Mom helps herself to a cube of tofu and another slice of meat, placing them on top of her rice, then placing the whole thing carefully in her mouth, chewing and swallowing.

"You're a very good doctor, Jin," she murmurs in Chinese, looking up finally. "I told you that you were wasted in that pretentious yum cha joint, that it would end badly, and it has. Do what you were born to do—make sick people better. Whatever way you can." Mom looks up at Dad and I can see that her chopstick hand is shaking, but her voice isn't. "There's no shame in that—in helping people."

Dad makes a sound like a roaring scream that rises and rises in scale and volume. He turns and storms back into his bedroom, slamming the door. My fists are still so tightly clenched that they *hurt* as I listen to him upending things in there, pounding on the walls, the doors, kicking and smashing things around. Working things out in the only way he knows how.

Across the table, Mom continues, calmly, to eat, although the hand cradling her bowl of rice is shaking. When she speaks again, her voice is thick and strange.

"I am sick of living as if I am seated on a carpet of needles. If I'd known what he was like before I married him, I'm not sure any of this would have been worth it—except for you. But this is the choice I made, no one else, and I have to live with it."

There's a tiny tear on Mom's cheek as she says this, and my throat is tight and very sore as Mom adds, "Eat, Wen. You have an important exam on Saturday."

Friday is a blur of nerves and uneasiness. Dad doesn't come out of his bedroom at all before Mom and I leave for school. It's as if the fact that Mom has a job now, and I've got an important exam tomorrow, is something that he can look away from. As if maybe if he doesn't come out of his room, none of it will be true.

"There's food in the fridge," Mom says tersely as we pick up Henry's last batch of homework from his doorstep on the way to school. "I've left your father a note again. And if he doesn't like what I've prepared for him, he is welcome to cook something else for himself. He is not going to starve."

There's bitterness in that word, *starve*.

I look at Mom with incredulity. I've never even seen Dad turn on the stove. He can barely work the microwave. One of us is always handing him a hot drink, or a bowl of nuts, or plate of cut-up fruit, when he's home. He doesn't have to lift a finger.

Time seems to run faster all day, faster than usual. Everyone except Billy Raum wishes me luck, and people keep giving me helpful advice like *Read the questions* and *Make sure you wear a watch* and *Don't eat too much for breakfast, you'll get gas.*

Michaela, Fatima and Nikki force me to sit in the sun with them instead of doing any more last-minute studying in the library.

"You've done enough," Fatima says firmly, taking out her lunchbox and starting to eat, her long-lashed dark eyes not leaving mine for a second.

"More than," Michaela adds, retouching the banged-up orange nail polish on her right thumb before studying the paint job critically with narrowed eyes.

"Homework with lashings of extra homework on top? Ugh," Nikki says, slipping me a book of poetry from our local secondhand book store. I recognize the stamp inside, underneath which she's written *You will smash it, girl.*

I give her a hug and she hugs me back, hard.

"I'm afraid," I mumble into her hair.

Of change, of leaving.

Of no change, of not leaving.

"You're allowed to feel and do anything you want," Nikki says fiercely, pushing back from me and staring into my face.

"Except kill someone," Michaela drawls, capping her nail polish bottle.

"Or set fire to school property," Fatima adds, snapping her lunchbox shut.

"Except maybe that." Nikki grins.

And it occurs to me, as the bell goes and the sick feeling in my chest that's been there all day returns, that they made me forget it for a little while.

Dad doesn't come out of his bedroom when I get back from school. He doesn't come out when Mom returns home from work, and he doesn't come out for dinner.

Later, when I'm in bed, unable to sleep because tomorrow is the day I'll be exposed as the fraud that Billy Raum has told everyone I am, I hear them talking in low voices on the other side of the wall between our rooms. I pretend I'm asleep as Dad moves down the hall slowly towards the kitchen. As I hear the sound of the microwave door popping open, I'm still pretending so hard to be asleep that I *am* asleep, even before the cycle of warming food finishes with a beep.

At precisely 7:15 on Saturday morning, Henry's dad's battered vegetable truck pulls into our driveway, the mashed leaves of vegetables and the remains of old fruit stuck to the sides of the deep metal tray at the back. Maybe the front curtain of our house twitches a little when Mom walks me and my cartoon-character-covered exam pencil case out to the cab of the truck. But that's all.

Mr. Xiao leaps out of the driver's seat to open the door for me. "Henry!" he says sharply. "Come down and thank Mrs. Zhou properly."

Through the windscreen, Henry's small face looks very pale, and I can't see his eyes behind his glasses because the morning sun is flaring in them.

Henry climbs slowly down out of the truck, clutching his own flat tin pencil case with all his exam stationery no doubt neatly arrayed inside in size and color order. He's wearing one of the new jumpers and a pair of the trousers that Nikki's and Fatima's families collected for him, but he's still got his terrible white runners on—the ones with the rips and holes all along the sides of the toes that let you see what color socks he's wearing.

Today, he's wearing one yellow sock and one red sock. They're awful. But the colors are lucky and bright and maybe that's why he chose them. Red for fortune, yellow for power.

I grin. Lucky socks.

I've got lucky socks on too. And lucky underwear. And a lucky jade necklace with a pendant on it in the shape of a heart. I'm not usually superstitious, but today is different. Maybe Henry—all scientific and logical and precise—is a little bit superstitious too.

Henry stops in front of Mom and just bows deeply, from the waist, without saying a word.

It's the kind of bow you'd do at a wedding, or at a funeral.

"*Henry*," his dad whispers beseechingly. "Please *say* something."

But Mom stops Mr. Xiao with a raised hand. "It was my great pleasure, Henry." She addresses him in formal Chinese, as if Henry has just spoken politely to thank Mom for all the hasty meals, all the hasty care that we could manage and arrange under the circumstances. "Now you and Wen go and make your parents very, very proud."

On the way to the school by the sea, we listen to crackly news radio and don't speak.

Mr. Xiao gets lost at one point and we have to turn into a side street so that he can puzzle over his cracked old phone and reorientate himself. I bet this wide street full of huge, leafy trees and graceful old houses with high fences has never had a big, dirty vegetable truck parked in it before, ever.

When we reach the school with a good half hour to spare, Mr. Xiao tells us that he will be right here, waiting outside when we're done.

"You read everything carefully, son," he says in

Chinese. "You answer every question until there is no space left to write things in. You hear me?"

Henry, staring down into the footwell of the truck, nods and nods as his dad speaks. I wonder if Henry has spoken to him at all since he found his mom in the apple tree.

As we climb out of the vegetable truck, Mr. Xiao gives us a little toot on the horn.

All the kids and parents filing into the school reception area look around at us and I glare back at them, my anger rising. *Everyone has to eat. And everyone's vegetables have to come from somewhere, you snobby old so-and-sos.*

There's a sharp tug on my sleeve and I turn, surprised.

"Just remember the remainder," Henry says in English, beside me. His voice still sounds rusty and unused, hesitant; the *R*s all optional, as usual.

For a second, I'm completely puzzled by Henry's advice. The rule is now burned into my memory as if it's somehow carved there. I don't think I will ever forget the remainder again, or how to do long division, until the day I die.

"I did all that on purpose, you know," I reply in English. "Just to annoy you."

Henry laughs in surprise, and his laughter sounds

rusty too. "Just don't annoy *them* the way you annoyed me, and you're going to do fine."

It occurs to me that Henry's still speaking in English. I'm not having to remind him to practice. He's doing it all by himself, and I know that he's *on*. He's in the zone. He's back, with his thinking cap on and game face ready.

"You're going to be finer than fine," I tell him. "It's in the bag. But good luck anyway."

"What is this 'bag' of which you speak?" Henry replies airily, with a grin. "Anyway, don't need it. See you in a couple of hours."

As soon as the exam finishes, I can't remember anything about it, any of the questions or what I thought or wrote after seeing them. I just feel really hungry as I look around for Henry.

He's sitting in the second row, right under the clock—probably so that he wouldn't miss, or waste, a second of available writing time. I bet he smashed it.

In the vegetable truck, driving home, all I can think about is what there might be to eat in the fridge but that I'm not sure I want to go home to eat it.

"Did you answer A or D to the question with the graph in it?" Henry says suddenly over the sound of the news radio. "That one is still bugging me."

I grin. When Henry uses slang, it sounds really wrong. "I honestly don't remember," I say, puzzled. "Was there even a graph question?"

Henry looks at me incredulously and I laugh. "All I can think about is a roast pork bāo, to be honest. Three, actually. I could inhale at least three."

"I'm thinking about a huge plate of gān chǎo níu hé." Henry grins back at me and I sigh out loud at the thought. Dry flash-fried beef rice noodles is one of my favorite dishes too.

"Good choice," I say approvingly as my stomach rumbles. "With extra onions, please."

But Henry's face suddenly falls and I say hastily, "When you win that place, we'll go out and order exactly that. At least half a dozen roast pork buns dripping with honey glaze, and a huge plate of fried rice noodles loaded with beef and onions for us to share."

"Yeah," Henry says flatly, and his dad gives him a sharp sideways glance. "Let's do that. When we win."

When we reach home, Mom shoots out of the front door as if she has springs in her legs and feet.

"So?" she enquires eagerly. "It went well?"

"I think it went . . . okay?" I say, because I still really can't remember a single thing I did after they told us to start writing.

Frustrated at the lack of detail, Mom turns to Henry. "Easy?" she says in Chinese.

Henry shrugs. "I was prepared," he replies quietly in the same language. "I was not surprised by anything."

His voice is still so flat and expressionless that he sounds like a robot, and Mom and I exchange anxious glances. It will be very hard to shock Henry Xiao ever again, I'm imagining.

"Come on, Henry," his dad says gently. "Let's go home now. You need to rest. It's been a busy few days."

It's a typically Chinese-style understatement, because it's probably been the biggest two weeks of Henry's life. You would never wish for bigger. Not even for your worst enemy.

Our screen door slams loudly and we all look up as my dad comes towards us in his disreputable sleep suit and indoor slippers, his hair hastily smoothed down with water but his face unshaven and lined. He looks old and careworn. Used up.

Like Pavlov's poor dog, I step back at the sight of him.

In the harsh sun, as he approaches, for the first time I feel shame at the way he is. I think about the pressed business shirts and trousers he used to wear, the pairs of leather business shoes that were so shiny you could see your face in them, and I wonder where that dad has gone. Was that dad *better* than this one? The too-neat, tightly wound-up dad who knew everything and was always roaring at me to *Do things properly!* versus this sloppy, speechless and sullen dad?

Dad reaches Mom, putting a heavy hand on her shoulder from behind as he studies Henry and his dad in silence.

"Mr. Zhou," Henry's dad says, ducking his head respectfully. "I must thank you . . ."

There's some kind of struggle going on behind Dad's rumpled face; I'm having trouble watching it. Mr. Xiao's words falter to a stop as he tries to read my dad's shifting expression.

"Uh, Bà," Henry says to his dad hastily in Chinese. "We should get going. We've bothered Mr. Zhou and Mrs. Zhou quite long enough . . ."

The silence is drawn out and awkward as Dad continues to stand there, studying us as if he's never seen any of us before, not even me.

When he speaks, I feel as if I'm dropping down into my body from a great and *whooshing* height, and I realize that I've been holding my breath for so long that I've grown dizzy. The ground seems to ripple under my shoes.

"Mr. Xiao," Dad says formally in Chinese. "I am deeply sorry for your loss. Please come inside and share a cup of tea with us before you go. Mei will prepare some food for us, a small snack, if you'd care to share that too?"

"She is a very fine cook," Mr. Xiao says gratefully, with a touch of surprise.

"Yes, she is," Dad agrees readily. "I'm very . . . lucky."

Mr. Xiao stiffens at the words, unsure of their exact meaning or intention, but he follows Dad up onto the front porch anyway.

Henry and I trail behind the adults, open-mouthed and goggling at each other, as we all enter my house.

Later that night, Henry and I sit out on the front porch, our feet and legs hanging down the steps, moths and gnats dive-bombing the light above our heads.

It has transpired, on this day of surprises, that the Zhou and Xiao families not only shared a soup noodle lunch that Mom hastily threw together, but also shared an evening meal of six dishes over rice, which was the lucky number Mom managed to eke out of her last round of food shopping. All of us crowded around our cramped kitchen table, sitting on mismatched chairs.

Between the two meals, our dads sat in the lounge room all afternoon and talked and talked over endless cups of cooling tea. Mom had put a finger to her lips and shooed us out each time we tried to go in to raid the pantry for anything resembling snack food. Something that will hopefully change now that Mom is working at the pharmacy with its copious display racks of jelly beans, raspberry drops and licorice allsorts that threaten to go out of date all the time, and must be eaten.

Mom told us to leave the dads to it.

"I have *you*, Wen," Mom said quietly as she looked down at Henry and me playing cards on my bedroom floor: endless games of Spit and Speed, gin rummy and Old Maid. "And Mrs. Xenakis, Dr. Gupta, all the old people. And you two have school, and your friends— and your big dreams. Let them talk in peace and find a new shape for their lives—the way we are all doing."

"Nikki is having a birthday party on Sunday, at the scout hall," I tell Henry now as he brushes an inquisitive moth away from his face. "I'm sure she'd love you to go."

Henry makes a huffing noise. "What would *I* do at a party?"

"Feel joy," I say simply. "Or boredom. Normal things. At least you wouldn't be hungry, or alone."

"It's been the worst two weeks of my life," Henry murmurs suddenly. "I can't even cry. It just sits in here."

He puts a closed fist against the front of his shirt, lets it drop.

I wait for him to say more, but he blinks behind his smudged glasses and looks down at his new trousers, picking at a loose thread that isn't even there.

"They were pretty bad for me, too," I say truthfully. "But nowhere near as bad as yours. I'm surprised our dads have so much to talk about, to be honest. They're very different."

"I'm surprised, too. We're common people," Henry murmurs. "Not like your dad, with all his degrees."

"There's nothing more common than a waiter in a restaurant," I say grimly. "There's nothing *special* about us. If Dad was special once, he's *chosen* to be common. It's on him. He's no better than your dad, for all his training and education. He turned his back on it. Why? Because his feelings were hurt. Because he couldn't compromise."

Henry turns to me now, frowning, the light bouncing off his spectacles and making his eyes unreadable again.

"What if we can't ever be anything more, or different, than what we are now?" he asks worriedly. "What if the exam, the idea of winning anything, is an illusion? How can we bear it, if it is?"

I take a deep breath, thinking quickly, knowing that what Henry is really talking about is his mom and why she chose not being here anymore over being with him.

I think what he's really asking is: *Is there a point to the struggle? Or are we just like these moths and gnats, bashing away at the bright lights and all the hard, fixed things, all the obstacles, until we are burnt out, and then we die anyway?*

"*All* of it is the point," I tell Henry urgently. "What you get out of it is the point. It's not about . . ." I think hard. ". . . reaching some kind of once-off pinnacle of luck or excellence or power—everything changes, all the time. It's like those waves I almost drowned in at Cape Schanck, you remember?"

Henry nods. He was one of the first ones in the water, forming a human chain to get me and the student teacher out of the pounding surf. "It's aiming for the peaks," I tell him, "and swimming through the troughs so that there are moments where you can just float under the sun and see how far you've come. Until you get pounded again. And then you have to start over."

"It's about never giving up, even if there's no point?" Henry says, brow furrowed.

Trust Henry to get to the heart of the problem and summarize it so succinctly.

"Yes," I agree softly. "The point is *how* you get to the point."

Henry's face clears; then he laughs.

From inside the house, I hear a bustle of movement, of voices raised in farewell. Henry's dad putting his faded old work boots on by the door, my dad telling him to give him a call next week because *I have contacts who can help you.*

Dad helping someone else, again? I crinkle my nose in wonder. Day of wonders, indeed.

Henry stands as someone unlocks the front door behind us.

"Thank you," he says to me simply, in Chinese, looking down at me through a halo of moths and gnats. "I will never forget, not even when I am old, what you have done for me."

"The point is how you get to the point," I remind him lightly, in English, although I feel like crying. I raise my fist in the same victory salute Henry gave me Wednesday night as he and his dad walk away down the footpath.

"This is why I will never get an A in English," Henry mock-grumbles over his shoulder.

I'm still seated on the top step as Henry and his dad drive away in their rattling truck. Behind me, Mom and Dad are silent for a long time. For once, it doesn't feel like a bad silence. It's not fraught with anything.

"Time for bed, Wen," Dad says finally as Mom puts a hand on my shoulder. "It seems that we have a birthday party to attend tomorrow."

As I turn and look up at them in delight, Dad smiles for the first time in days.

CODA

The spirit of the valley never dies
This is called the mysterious female.
The gateway of the mysterious female
Is called the root of heaven and earth.
Dimly visible, it seems as if it were there,
Yet use will never drain it.

— Lao Tzu, Tao Te Ching, Book 1, VI

AUTHOR'S NOTE

I often tell people who don't know me very well that I am made of questions, and of coffee.

I drink so much coffee that my heart rate—when I'm sitting down—is probably the same as your heart rate when you're winning a 100-meter race.

If you do know me well, though, you'll know that one of my favorite things is to ask, *But why?*

I question everything I come into contact with. Ideas, systems, stories, people.

It was the way I tackled things that didn't make sense to me when I was a little girl, and it's the way I still approach things today: *Why is something "true"? Is it really "true" or have we just accepted the "truth" of it because that's just how people have always done it? If it's not "true" and it's unfair, or even wrong, why can't we change it? Why can't we do something else? Why can't we do something* better?

If you recognize yourself in Wen at all, if you understand that the whole of *Tiger Daughter* is really one big *but why?* question—that it's me thinking out loud and advocating to keep what's good, what's benevolent, but to discard ideas and systems and behaviours that hold us back—I'm telling you that *I see you.*

You are not alone. Things *will* change. Things will not always seem so narrow and impossible and immutable.

One day you *will* be free—but it will be up to you to push back, to step outside the boundaries that other people have drawn out for you, to see over the edges of the box, to think for yourself. No one can do that for you, but you.

Accept no limitations.

NOTE TO TEACHERS AND LIBRARIANS

A huge part of why I write, and why I create the kinds of books and stories that I do, is about building empathy in my readers. That's my guiding principle.

I was a migrant child of the 1970s and 1980s. Being Asian or migrant or refugee was certainly never positively portrayed or synonymous with being "Australian" back then. I never saw myself in any children's books from that time, and I have only just, in 2020, edited a picture book featuring a little Asian girl protagonist which was wholly written and illustrated by an Asian Australian author.

Tiger Daughter is the product of years of thinking and processing, and it's trying to work on a number of levels.

It's seeking to build that empathy in readers, but it's also interrogating things that humanity is currently grappling with—racism, sexism, violence against women and girls, financial abuse, intersectionality, superstition, systemic bias, unconscious bias, privilege, the mainstream idea of what is "normal"—through the story of a migrant girl who has to resist these things while walking in two worlds: the mainstream "Western" sphere she is expected to navigate and accumulate fluency in, and the private, cultural sphere in which she is being brought up.

Tiger Daughter asks mainstream readers—readers who've never been told to "go back where you come from," and never will be—to think about what it would feel like to be marginalized for more reasons than merely being female.

Tiger Daughter is also, most defiantly, not a book that assumes anything. It does not assume that the reader and writer share an identical background that is somehow "universal," homogenous and instantly translatable. It does not assume that the reader's and the writer's ways of thinking, their philosophies, their belief systems or their conditions of life are the same, because they can't be. While it can't speak for, or to, everyone who is migrant or refugee, *Tiger Daughter* is a migrant story for children actually written by a migrant. Not someone "imagining," from inside their relative privilege, what it would feel like to be one. And that makes *Tiger Daughter* if not unique, then sadly still too rare.

As recently as the first COVID-19 lockdown in March 2020, I was subjected to racial abuse by the family members of a neighbor while standing in the "safety" of my own garden. Even though I worked then as a commercial lawyer in one of the biggest law firms in the country, that feeling—of being an outsider— never ever goes away. Not for me, and not, I imagine, for any migrant or refugee Australian. There is not one day where I am not intensely aware of relative levels of privilege, and I am always working to ensure that in my dealings with First Nations people, with People of Color, with people of every kind there is, I am doing the right thing.

Tiger Daughter is about one girl's small quest to do the right thing, despite having no power or privilege. I really hope it speaks to you and to the children in your lives who are processing and grappling with the same big issues that we are.

ABOUT THE AUTHOR

Rebecca Lim is an award-winning Australian writer, illustrator, and editor and the author of more than twenty books, including *Tiger Daughter* and the best-selling *Mercy*. Her work has won the Children's Book Council of Australia's Book of the Year Award for Older Readers and the Victorian Premier's Literary Award, and has been longlisted for the Gold Inky Award and the David Gemmell Legend Award. It has also been shortlisted for the Prime Minister's Literary Awards, the New South Wales Premier's Literary Awards, the Queensland Literary Awards, the Margaret and Colin Roderick Literary Award, and the INDIEFAB Book of the Year Awards, and has been shortlisted multiple times for the Aurealis Award and the Davitt Award. Her novels have been translated into German, French, Turkish, Portuguese, Polish, and Russian. She is a co-founder of the Voices from the Intersection initiative and coeditor of *Meet Me at the Intersection*, a ground-breaking anthology of YA memoir, poetry, and fiction.